PUSHKI

TOSHIYUKI HORIE (born 1964) is a scholar of French literature and a professor at Waseda University. He has won many literary prizes, including the Mishima Yukio Prize, Akutagawa Prize (for *The Bear and the Paving Stone*), the Kawabata Yasunari Prize, the Tanizaki Jun'ichiro Prize and the Yomiuri Prize for Literature (twice).

TOSHIYUKI HORIE

THE
BEAR
AND THE
PAVING
STONE

translated by
GERAINT HOWELLS

PUSHKIN PRESS

SERIES EDITORS: David Karashima and Michael Emmerich
TRANSLATION EDITOR: Elmer Luke

Pushkin Press
Somerset House, Strand
London WC2R 1LA

"The Bear and the Paving Stone" with the title "Kuma no shikiishi"
first appeared in the Japanese literary magazine *Gunzo* in 2000

"The Sandman Is Coming" with the title "Sunauri ga toru" first
appeared in the Japanese literary magazine *Shincho* in 2000

"In the Old Castle" with the title "Shiroato nite" first appeared
in the Japanese literary magazine *Shincho* in 1999

Copyright © Toshiyuki Horie 1999 and 2000

English translation rights arranged with Toshiyuki Horie
through Japan Foreign-Rights Centre

English translation © Geraint Howells 2018

First published by Pushkin Press in 2018

The publisher gratefully acknowledges the support of the
British Centre for Literary Translation and the Nippon Foundation

3 5 7 9 8 6 4

ISBN 13: 978-1-78227-437-7

Designed and typeset in Marbach by Tetragon, London
Printed and bound in the United Kingdom by Clays Ltd, Elcograf S.p.A.

www.pushkinpress.com

CONTENTS

THE BEAR
AND
THE PAVING STONE

AT SOME POINT, I GOT LOST. The mountains were gloomy, the sun just about to set, and I'd suddenly emerged on to a path that was covered in a strange kind of undergrowth, hard like artificial grass, jutting out at sharp angles, yet somehow soft at the same time. There was the faint smell of animals. I thought I could feel their body heat—maybe there was an animal trail nearby. Stumbling across this path was surely a stroke of luck, and though my legs had become numb with fatigue, they could probably keep me going. If worse came to worst, I could light a fire and spend the night right here. The very next moment, however, the ground started to move beneath me, like a carpet of giant black caterpillars, and I lost my footing. I fell on to my bottom, and the ground started to undulate, poking into me. Shocked and frightened, I got up and set off running blindly through the trees, forgetting how tired I was. The next thing I knew I was at the top of a slightly elevated outcrop. Breathing heavily, I looked down at what had, until a few hours previously, been a kind of paradise. The soft jet-black path had swollen into a rocky fortress. I strained to see better, and discovered that the path was actually a countless number of bears, standing on their hind legs, huddled together in formation. They seemed to be moving as one, making their way into the mountains. What's going on? Had I been walking on the backs of those bears? Running on a carpet of their hair, thick with bitumen, here and there matted in hard clumps? I was covered in sweat, but I'd lost my towel while I was running, so I couldn't dry off. I stood there dumbfounded while the bears jostled their way into the distance. Just then, a breeze carrying a fishy tidal smell came wafting from the middle of the sea of black ursine bodies, where a solitary, slightly unbalanced triangular island now appeared. I was wheezing from the exertion, and this thick, warm, salty air was blocking my airways. My throat started to hurt. I wanted some water. I wanted something cool. I looked around, and my eyes fell upon a spring sputtering out of a crack in the rock face just beneath me. Unsteadily, I crouched down and scooped some up in my hands, lifting it to my lips. Immediately, there was a gloopy sweet taste in my mouth, followed by a chill that stung the back of my throat and sent sharp, stabbing pains to the molar that I'd been too lazy to take care of. I cried out. I forgot about my thirst, about the carpet of bears, and lay down on the ground. It was all I could do to endure the intense pain in my mouth.

Through the hole in the wooden shutters, a diamond of soft sunlight shone on to the unglazed tile floor. The air in the room was fresh and clean—in fact, it was almost cool—but my body was burning up. I was also thirsty, and my right molar ached, just like it had in the dream. I wasn't sure if this was because of how I was lying on the sofa bed—with my face squashed against the back of the sofa because the bed part wouldn't open out—or because of the dream itself, which had been eerily vivid. I looked at the clock on the table. It was already half past nine. I hadn't heard Yann leave. I got up slowly and went to the bathroom, found some aspirin in the medicine cabinet—who knows how long they'd been there—and tossed a couple of tablets into a cup of water. I watched as the bubbles rushed noisily to the surface. I drank the medicine down, and it stung my tongue. Praying for relief from the pain, I turned the shower on and got under a lukewarm spray.

From the small top-hinged window, I could see a fence of wooden posts pounded into the ground at random intervals. There was no barbed wire between them, just a single thick wire that drooped untidily, like a telephone line. Apparently the nearest neighbours, who owned the vast shrub-filled land, lived on the other side of some far-off hills. There really wasn't any sign of anyone else living around here at all.

The bathroom had been built by the previous owner, a DIY buff. The floor tiles were uneven, and so water easily overflowed the drain and wet the whole bathroom floor. Still waking up, I tried my best to control the flow. My towel got soaked, and it made me think of the black carpet of bears in my dream.

I'd driven to this remote farmhouse in Normandy, speeding along gently undulating country roads lined with low trees, passing bare fields of freshly harvested wheat and pastures of cows grazing under layers of cloud. It was pure happenstance that I was here. I'd been visiting Paris after many years. I had some work I needed to do, and as a result, I spent most of my days alone. I'd wanted to see friends I used to hang out with, but most had proper jobs now and I was hesitant to get in touch during the heavy period just before their summer holidays. Eventually, I managed to get most of my work done, and found myself with a bit of free time. That was when I thought of Yann, who was a perpetual freelancer, unbound by a company schedule. I hadn't heard anything from him for two years, so I tried ringing him at his parents' home. His father, whom I'd met on several occasions, answered the phone. His voice became animated when I introduced myself. He remembered me well. We chatted for a while, then I asked if he knew how I could reach Yann as he never replied to my letters. His father laughed, saying that Yann never wrote to his parents either. Then he told me that Yann had left Paris two years ago and had put down anchor in a small village in Normandy.

"I've never visited, so I don't know what kind of house it is," he said. "It sounds like it's really in the sticks, though."

He gave me Yann's number and advised me to call late as otherwise he probably wouldn't be there. I knew that Yann worked part-time a few months a year, and used the money he earned to travel and take photos, but I hadn't expected him to move out of his studio in the Paris suburbs—it'd been perfect for him. I waited until much later that night before ringing, only to get the answering machine on every try. I finally left him a message with my hotel phone number, and early the next morning Yann called, his voice sounding quite like his father's, just a little higher.

"I'm sorry," he began. "I got all your letters. They were forwarded to me. I should have replied, but there's been a lot going on." And then he told me he was going to Ireland the next morning and would be there for twenty days.

I only had two weeks before I needed to head home, so if we were going to meet, it had to be today.

"I'd like to go and meet you in Paris right now," Yann said, "but I need to sort out my travel plans and stuff. If it's OK with you, how about we meet somewhere outside Paris? Caen, maybe? It takes about two hours by train. I can drive there in about ninety minutes, if I put my foot down. We'll have something to eat, and this way we'll at least get to see each other."

If we missed this chance, we probably wouldn't meet again for several years. I didn't have any plans that after-noon, and a two-hour train ride to spend the day with a friend didn't seem like a bad idea. The only work I still had to do was a synopsis of a novel that might be translated, but I could do that anywhere. In fact, a change of scene could even boost my productivity. I didn't bother checking out of my hotel, and just packed a rucksack. I went to the station and bought a ticket, then I called Yann to let him know when I'd be arriving.

It was the weekend, and the train was crowded. I read for a while, but then a tall student joined me in my compartment. We exchanged a few words, and before long he was telling me about his hometown, Villedieu-les-Poêles—it turned out that he was on his way there. *Ville* means "town", *dieu* means "God", and *poêle* means "pan", so I asked him if this was a town where God had fried something in a pan. He chuckled, then explained that *poêle* can refer to copper products in general, and that the town had been at the heart of France's metalwork industry for centuries. Even though there were no copper mines in the area, it had become famous as the place where the bronze for the country's church bells was cast. As we were talking, a little boy who'd been poking his head into every compartment in the carriage took an interest in us, and without hesitation sat himself down. He was called Iywan, an old Norman name, and once the ice was broken, he started talking to us as if we were old friends. We ended up talking with him for a long time, answering every question he asked. We played a game where we were supposed to guess who he was thinking about. He'd give us hints that didn't make any sense and

sit there laughing to himself, and then change the subject completely and start talking about school. He declared proudly that he had a computer and that he took three different sports classes a week. He also said he wasn't interested in regular girls—only *filles de passion*. He then blushed, and I made a mental note that this word was now in the vocabulary of primary school children in the countryside. When I told him I was from Japan, he looked shocked, and asked me, repeatedly, why my eyes weren't slanted upwards. I told him that there were all sorts of faces in the world—some with eyes that slanted upwards, others with eyes that drooped down.

"Your eyes look like this," I told him, pulling at the corner of my eyes to slant them downwards. He didn't respond to this. Instead he leaned against the armrest of the seat, swinging his legs, and announced, apropos of nothing, that when he grew up he was going to be a veterinarian or a computer scientist.

"Veterinarians and computer scientists are pretty different—" I began to say.

"Well, I'm going to be a veterinarian or a computer scientist," he said quickly. Maybe he thought he was being made fun of, as he soon stood up and walked out of our compartment.

"Kids in Normandy tend to like animals, so lots of them want to be veterinarians," the student said. "When I was a kid, I wanted to be a veterinarian or a fireman." He smiled gently, as though he were making excuses for the boy. "Everyone's got a dream," he added.

This reminded me of something I'd happened to see on TV at the hotel—a currant-picking contest—and I decided to tell the student about it. The contest was to see who could pick the most currants within a given time-limit. Contestants had to use tweezers, and they had to be careful not to crush the currants. It was a local event in this village, and an old woman was the winner. Apparently her mother had won the championship years before, so she was delighted she could write the names of two generations of her family in the history books. It had been her dream. Everybody indeed does have one, it seemed.

"I had a friend whose dream was to win the Camembert-throwing championship," the student said.

"A Camembert-throwing championship?"

"We lived in a dairy-farming area. We'd take an old Camembert and throw it like a discus, competing to see who could get it the furthest."

An image floated into my mind: a beautiful ancient Greek statue of a man, knees bent slightly, preparing to launch his discus.

"And did your friend achieve his dream?"

"He did."

"What was the winning distance."

"57.38 metres."

I fell silent. The men's discus world record must have been something like that, and even though a Camembert didn't weigh as much as a two-kilo discus, 57 metres was still an incredible distance. And there was no way that he

could have cheated. If he'd turned away from the judges in a crouch and nibbled the cheese to make it lighter, his deception would have been revealed as soon as the Camembert hit the ground. He'd thrown it that far, fair and square. I imagined the Camembert catching a breeze and sailing in a majestic arc across the sky, and I felt strangely moved. Then, still thinking about the cheese, I stood up, shook hands with my good-natured student friend and got off the train. I'd reached my destination. Just after three in the afternoon, Yann and I were reunited.

There was quite a crowd of passengers, but he managed to spot me, and raised his hand in greeting. The little bit of hair he'd once had was gone, and his scalp gleamed with an almost pure white light. In addition to shaving his head, he'd had the lobes of his distinctively pointy ears pierced and was sporting a pair of earrings that I could never have imagined him wearing before. The shape of his head seemed chiselled, with his deep eye sockets—though that may have been because the exit from the station was in the shade. It had been many years since we'd last seen each other, and so things were a little awkward at first, but after I'd got into the passenger seat of his pickup truck, it soon started to feel like old times and all the blank years in between just disappeared.

"It must be about five years since we had a proper chat," I said.

Yann took one hand off the steering wheel, and wagged his index finger. He made a theatrical clucking sound with his tongue. "I've been thinking about when we last spoke," he said. "It was before you went back to Japan. You called me from some hotel."

In which case, it must have been even longer since we'd seen each other.

"I'd just started that job at the quarry. Do you remember? I took all those photos of stones and brought them to show you."

"Yeah. You gave me a photo as a farewell gift actually. It was a close-up shot, but I didn't really understand it. It was of this big stone wall, with the stones joined together roughly. It wasn't a photographic print, though. It was photocopied, but the quality was really good."

"Yeah, in those days I used the photocopier's 'photo mode' to save money. And I think I took that photo in one of the old quarries from this area. There's a granite quarry and factory not so far from my house. The granite industry is on its last legs now, but it won't be allowed to die out completely—they wouldn't be able to repair the pavements in the big cities if it did. I still work there sometimes. I don't get paid, though. The workers let me take their photos instead."

His voice and his accent were exactly the same as I remembered, but the rays of sunlight that were popping out between the clouds and catching on his silver earrings were putting me on edge. We'd been driving around near the station, looking for somewhere inviting to eat. The area was full of cheap-looking restaurants designed to attract summer tourists, and their terraces were deserted now that the lunch hour was over. The main shopping street looked like it had been built from papier mâché. Nowhere looked like a very good place to eat.

"Whose bright idea was it to meet here...?" I said, half-joking.

I was obviously feeling comfortable enough with Yann if I could say something like this. But it turned out that Yann himself had hardly visited the town either, so he knew about as much as I did.

"Still, if this is a station on a main rail line, why is it so bleak around here?" I now asked.

"Most of the buildings were bombed during the war. The town tried to restore them, but they could only manage this fake stuff. It could be a lot worse, you know," Yann replied very seriously. Then, after a pause, he said, "It's a shame you don't have more time. You could have come to my place. Actually, though, why don't you just come anyway and catch the last train back? Or if you don't have to go back to your hotel tonight, you could stay the night and leave with me first thing in the morning. You could even stay longer, if you like. It's a great place for writing. Quiet."

"Writing" wasn't quite an accurate word for what I did. I did piecework, translating a part of a book and then writing a synopsis of the plot so that an editor could decide whether to publish the full translation. Since arriving in Paris, I'd finished off two synopses of novels that I wasn't feeling very enthusiastic about. In any case, all I had in my rucksack, apart from the essentials, was a concise

French-Japanese dictionary, another book I really didn't need to rush with, and a notebook. This was supposed to be only a day trip, so I hadn't even packed a change of clothes. But my interest had been piqued by the granite factory that Yann seemed to know well, and so I started to think that if I could check the place out, I wouldn't mind extending my stay a bit.

"Are we going past the quarry and the factory?"

"Sure. We probably can't go in, though, because it's the weekend. Anyway, shall we?"

I hesitated for a while, then told him that I was game. There's nothing wrong with breathing a bit of fresh country air from time to time. We'd been travelling in pretty much a straight line, but when Yann heard my response he put his foot down and made a sharp turn. I felt the kind of G-force you feel when riding the tea cups, and in the blink of an eye, my surroundings had changed. Yann's earrings jangled, and his camera, which he'd placed on the dashboard, crashed to the floor. The camera was Yann's livelihood, but he seemed totally unperturbed as he reached out one hand to pick it up. To check it was still working he clicked the shutter, which made a soft abrasive sound like a magician cutting a deck of cards, then he handed it to me, asking me to hold it for him. He gunned the engine, and off we went, unobstructed views in every direction. There were no large buildings to be seen, but the sky was covered with low flat clouds, and I didn't quite get the sense of release I'd been expecting. Yann was telling me all about the local terrain and the history of the nearby villages as he drove. He sounded like a geography teacher.

After about half an hour on a main road that cut through the middle of some wheat fields, Yann said, "This is actually the place I was planning on coming to after putting you on the train back to Paris. Would you mind if we stopped here now? It won't take long."

All of a sudden, we pulled over on the side of the road—there was no hard shoulder. Yann grabbed his camera and, with barely any concern for the trucks that were flying past us, dashed across the road and scrambled up a mound covered with dead grass. I didn't like being left behind, so I summoned up some rash courage and ran across the road after him. We were at the edge of a vast wheat field. In one corner were three rusty water tanks, each about two metres tall. Yann climbed on to the one on the right, and trained his lens on the bales of hay dotting the field. They were all about the same size, which suggested the work of experienced hands, but they varied slightly in shape. Sometimes they slumped a bit, or had indentations. There seemed, at a glance, to be over a hundred bales, and whenever the sun was blocked by the clouds, their golden hue would darken and they would suddenly resemble a still, soundless herd of bison. After about fifteen minutes, Yann climbed down from the water tank. He said that he'd last taken photos here the previous winter. The field had been covered in snow, and there was an old tractor crawling along, spewing out smoky exhaust fumes. He was planning to do a kind of time-lapse series, it seemed, observing the passing of the seasons.

We went back to his truck, taking care now to look both ways before crossing the road. We set off again, heading off the main road on to a narrow lane that undulated gently. The hillsides were dense with the pastureland known as bocage—fields surrounded with low hedges that acted as windbreaks. In front of each house we passed were rectangular stones, not particularly big, stuck into the ground at regular intervals with trees planted in the gaps between them. Their roots would wrap themselves around the stones, Yann said, making the trees better able to withstand the wind.

Whenever we drove through a village, we were sure to find a stone church with a graveyard behind it; life and death coexisting snugly next to each other. One of these villages was on a bit of a hill, and Yann stopped in the square in front of the church, saying we should take a break. It seemed he'd been to this village before, and he led me to one corner of the square, drawing my attention to a sign that claimed this was the furthest point from which the spire of Mont Saint-Michel could be seen. Next to the sign were some stone stairs that led up to the kind of bog-standard observation deck you'd expect to find in a hilltop village like this. On a clear day, it supposedly offered a view of the majestic Gothic monastery, but today was not clear and I couldn't make anything out. I was surprised to realize that Yann's house was even further north than this village, with its view of Mont Saint-Michel. Until then I'd had the idea he lived in the hills, surrounded by orchards or fields full of livestock.

"Your father only told me your phone number, and then we arranged to meet in Caen, so I just never really thought about it, but I guess your house must be quite close to the sea?"

"Not really. It's just outside a little village, quite a way inland. You can see the sea from Avranches, though, and that's only a thirty-minute drive."

"Hold on, did you say Avranches? The Avranches where Littré's family came from?"

"Littré? The dictionary guy? Yeah, come to think of it, that's right. His family did come from there."

"Why didn't you tell me? I'd have come to your house right away if I knew it was near Avranches. I'll explain in a second."

We went back to the truck, where I took the book out of my rucksack and handed it to Yann. The cover was a copper-plate engraving of a man's portrait, and the book was a biography of Émile Maximilien Paul Littré, the man responsible for producing the many bulky volumes of the *Dictionnaire de la langue française* in the second half of the nineteenth century. It was the book I was reading and translating a part of. I'd thought it'd be convenient to have it along while on the move. Unlike a novel, which demands to be read in one sitting, a critical biography like this, divided into many sections, was something I could work through bit by bit. Avranches was a place name that had always had some kind of resonance for me (it sounded like *avouer*—to confess—and *blanchir*—to launder money—and it made me think of something slippery, like *abura*, the Japanese word for oil), but if I hadn't come across it in the introduction to the book I was working on, I'd never have connected it to Littré or Normandy.

"There's a high school in Avranches named after him, so I guess he's a kind of famous local person. I've actually got some of the *Littré* on the shelf at home—not a complete set, mind you. It was left there by the person who rented the place before me. In fact, some of the guys I met while working round here went to the Lycée Émile Littré. The school used to have a portrait of Littré in the assembly hall that was so ugly the students complained and the school eventually got rid of it. Pretty funny, eh?"

Littré may have been one of the giants of the nineteenth century, a man of knowledge and curiosity, but I couldn't blame those high school kids for wanting to get rid of the great man's portrait. His hair was always smoothed down over his narrow forehead, and he wore small, oval silver-framed spectacles, but he also had a massive lower lip which stuck out like a bullfrog's, and this was his most distinctive feature. Whenever there was a caricature of him, there was that big lower lip. There's probably no greater indignity than to have your entire existence rejected on account of your ugly face—especially by a bunch of students who still rely on your work. For me, though, the thought of spending some time near Avranches with a biography of Littré in hand had got me quite excited. I was long past the age when I enjoyed changing my plans suddenly, impetuously, without even a change of clothes, but being with Yann now, I was reminded of when I was clueless and new to France and he would take me to all sorts of different places to try and cheer me up.

Back then, Yann had also just started living by himself, so he was probably filled with a kind of eagerness or enthusiasm for life. But there's no doubt that what bonded us was mutual nervousness. Why else would Yann have asked me, out of the blue, to go for a meal with him in the Jewish quarter, insisting that he wanted me to eat a sandwich that was at least minimally Jewish? The way he spoke, it was as though he were persuading me to join a cult, and his invitation was half coercion, but at the time I didn't know that Yann was Jewish, and I had no idea where the Jewish quarter was or why he'd want to show me that neighbourhood. We set off in the evening, taking the metro to Saint-Paul, and went to a deli on the Rue des Rosiers that sold smoked meats and pickles, rye bread and Israeli red wine. The shop had once been targeted by Palestinian terrorists, who'd planted a bomb that left several casualties. Photos of the tragedy had been enlarged and printed on panels placed in the shop window, alongside photos of famous people. This gave me a real feeling for the shop's staying power, its determination to do business no matter what. The unconventional advertising seemed to be working too, as the shop had plenty of customers. There was a long line at the till that wasn't moving much, so to shorten our wait

I started queuing while Yann grabbed what we needed. When it was finally our turn, Yann announced that this was his treat, and he insisted on paying for everything. Standing behind him, I could see that he was surreptitiously holding a can of something under his arm. Once we were outside, Yann gave a proud little laugh, thrusting his nose into the cool evening air.

"I stole it, obviously," he explained.

"But you paid for everything else? You just stole this?"

"The stuff I paid for was cheap. This, I couldn't afford."

What he'd stolen was a can of grape leaves stuffed with rice, marinated in spices and olive oil. Even though I saw the label, I was so shocked that he hadn't paid for it that I couldn't remember what they were called. In those days, I felt very vulnerable in my status as a foreigner living in France, and I was supremely sensitive to the fact that I needed to avoid getting into any trouble with the authorities. I started thinking how bad it would be if Yann was caught and what my culpability in it all was. I felt angry, for selfish reasons, and struggled to control my anger. Then I relaxed. This was brazen shoplifting, but we were out of the shop and I couldn't have done anything to stop it.

We crossed the Seine to the Île de la Cité, and sat down on a bench. Yann took out butter, Gruyère and mineral water from his rucksack, and lined them up in front of us. He poured the wine into paper cups, and opened his shoplifted loot with a tin opener he'd brought with him—he'd clearly been meaning to steal the can all along. The stuffed grape leaves were delicious. The olive oil and the saltiness fit perfectly, and there was some vinegar in the marinade as well, which added a nice touch. Yann had warned me that there were people who couldn't eat the grape leaves, so I shouldn't force myself if I didn't like them. But once I'd had a couple, I knew that they were just the kind of thing I loved. We made sandwiches with the meats and pickles and chunks of black bread. There was a bit of an acrid taste, but it went really well with the dry, slightly sandy red wine. As we worked our way through our little feast, Yann told me that when he was a little boy his grandmother would sometimes take him shopping to the Rue des Rosiers. His grandmother on his mother's side was Polish, and his grandfather was Russian.

"Did you have a reason for taking me there?" I asked.

"I don't really know. It's not because you're a foreigner or anything. I can't really put it into words... but there's something about you, I knew you wouldn't take it the wrong way. I know you don't do judo or anything, but you know how to take a knock or two."

I wasn't sure, but I thought I understood when he said there was "something about me". That "something", whenever I met someone new, gave me a clue whether or not we'd be able to get to know each other. Usually, if don't I feel a connection with someone, I'll conclude that they're probably not someone I need in my life, and I'll stay away. But when I do connect with someone, the connection lasts, and it's a bit like the shell fire in that Kenji Miyazawa children's story. You don't fiddle with the flame. The flame has nothing to do with nationality, age, gender, status. When it's lit it's lit, and when it goes out it goes out, though its warmth might remain for a while. This "something about me", however, lent itself to other things. With Yann, I was his blank slate, someone in whom he had no stake, no self-interest to protect. So he could let his guard down. And I also got the sense that his deciding to tell me about his family was somehow related to his shoplifting performance. I think, looking back, that was the moment when I realized I trusted Yann. There were probably other customers who'd realized that Yann had hidden the can under his arm, but I was the person standing behind him, he was showing me what he was doing, and I didn't say anything, which meant I shared in the act—and the guilt. The feeling I now had, several years later, after "something about me" had led Yann to bring me to this corner of Normandy, was very similar to what I felt on that day.

In the square in front of the church there was a cafe, which also served as a news-stand and tobacco shop. We sat at one of the gloomy tables and ordered sandwiches. The old shopkeeper had used up all his baguettes at lunch, and so, after asking if we minded, cut some thick-crusted *pain de campagne*. He spread on fresh local butter and added slices of ham. We couldn't have asked for anything better.

After passing through a town—famous for its sausages, according to Yann—we drove along a winding road that meandered its way up and down hills and didn't offer much of a view of the surroundings. Eventually we emerged into a valley, a small river on our right. The landscape seemed noticeably drier, with less greenery and more white stone. Yann took this as his cue to tell me that the reason cider was produced in this area was because the water quality was so bad—people were better off drinking alcohol.

Soon we pulled up to the granite factory, which was alongside the river. As expected, no one was working because it was the weekend, and the gate was locked.

"Well, that's that. If you want to see what it's like inside, you'll have to make do with the photos at my place," Yann said, as he continued driving, not bothering to stop. He took a narrow country road that was surfaced with granite chippings, and we kept going on for another long while.

"I thought you told me it was ninety minutes from your place to Caen," I said, "but we've being going for a couple of hours."

"I didn't take this route on the way there," he replied. "It's not so far if you're on a proper road and you speed a little." Laughing, he continued on through a series of small bends, and eventually I could see dense forest up ahead.

Before long, Yann announced, "We're here!"

A pair of almost cubic stones, like gateposts, marked the entrance to his property. We drove past a wooden shed, which he said contained straw and firewood, and eventually a gabled dull brick building came into view.

"Welcome to chez Yann," Yann said, spreading his arms wide, then guiding me into a single room of about twenty-five square metres. In the right corner was a staircase leading to the loft, and directly in front of me was an imposing grandfather clock which the previous tenants had left behind and which seemed to have stopped working. A sofa and assorted pieces of furniture were carelessly placed around the room, all of which had apparently been scavenged. The fireplace on the left had a thick metal plate behind it that reflected heat back into the room, and a set of bellows lay in front of it. Both the metal plate and the bellows had been picked up from a demolition site, Yann said, as though this would be entirely obvious. Above the fireplace was a shield, awarded to finalists at the Île-de-France pétanque tournament. It looked like a mineral specimen, plonked unceremoniously on a shelf.

"The only thing in here I bought was the Marshall valve amp," Yann said.

I put down my stuff, and Yann took me out for a tour of the surroundings. It was quiet. The nearest neighbours, whose house was three hundred metres from the road, kept cows and chickens, but I couldn't hear nor see them. All I could hear was birdsong and the rustling of leaves, the murmuring of a brook and the crunching of gravel under our feet. In the apple and pear orchard, the previous tenants, an old couple who'd left the grandfather clock behind, had built a hut where they baked bread. The oven no longer worked, so it was useless, but according to Yann, it wasn't uncommon for people here to have a hut for baking the kind of crusty bread we'd eaten in the cafe. *Pain de campagne* might dry out, but when that happened you just cut it into pieces and put it in soup and it becomes a whole meal. At the end of the back garden, the boundary with the neighbours was marked with white objects that looked like broken pieces of china, but with cylindrical blue cores protruding out of them. They seemed most odd until Yann explained they were lumps of rock salt that the cows would sometimes come and lick. As he talked, he pulled a nearby branch that was laden with blackcurrants towards him, plucked some off and handed them to me. They were more acidic than the currants they sold at the market in Paris, but were refreshing and had no unpleasant aftertaste. I picked as many currants as I could hold in my handkerchief, and made some throwaway remark about having them with yogurt later.

Yann looked a bit embarrassed at this. "We should have stopped and got some supplies when we were passing through town. Since I'm leaving tomorrow, I was planning on eating out tonight. There's almost no food in the house."

He was right. Back in the kitchen, I saw that the fridge really was almost empty. Just some pickles and a jar of strawberry jam. On the shelf were several types of pasta, age unknown, and a bottle of bourbon someone had given him. Yann put a pot of water on the stove, then rummaged around in the drawer of the plywood dining table and pulled out two teabags. He popped them into a stained teapot, then added water once it had boiled. Elbowing the stuff on the table out of the way, he laid down two cracked yellow bowls.

"You've given up on jam jars, then?"

"What are you talking about?"

"You used to drink tea out of jam jars all the time, even though everyone thought that was weird."

"Ha. Well, I don't do dumb stuff like that any more. Besides, we both did dumb stuff when we were young."

I wasn't sure that it was all down to being young. Yann didn't get along with his parents very well back then, and was always in a bad mood. Maybe that's why he'd consciously do things that would grab people's attention. He used to carry around a folding penknife, as if he were some pre-war woodsman, and when we went to restaurants, he'd bring it out to cut his meat and fish. He used to burn incense, so that his room would always have a sickly sweet smell. And he used to call me in the middle of the night to go and play pétanque by street light. (In fact, that's how I first met him, at a pétanque tournament organized by some elderly people in the parish.) He wanted to buy an old van and travel all over France, so he handed out flyers to his friends asking them to provide funding. On other occasions, a thought would occur to him and he'd shut himself in his room for days, reading. Everyone knew about his thing with jam jars. Whenever he drank tea or *café au lait*, it'd be in a Bonne Maman jar—that was the most common brand—and he would refuse to drink out of anything else. His reason: one Bonne Maman jarful was just the right amount—any more and he wouldn't be able to sleep, any less and he'd still be thirsty. No one knew what to think of that. His grandmother would make marmalade and jam—apricot and quince—in used jars and seal them with wax. Yann always had several of these jars in his room, and the friends who hoped to be given one learned to stop mentioning Yann's habit of drinking out of them. Once, on a whim, I tried drinking tea out of a jar myself. It was too hot to hold, and the grooves for screwing on the cap made it not the easiest vessel to drink from.

We talked for a while, discussing things as they occurred to us, things that may or may not have actually happened. Yann knew the limits of my language ability, speaking more slowly and choosing his words more carefully than he might have done otherwise. A detail that could have been shared in seconds went on much longer, as though an older child were explaining something to a younger child. A lot of time passed without my noticing it. I went back over what I'd written in my letters. Yann hadn't got a regular job since we'd last met, nor had I. I'd made ends meet by doing piecemeal business-related translation work and part-time teaching jobs. Yann listened, and then, in his own entertaining way, told the story of how he ended up settling in the village.

One of the factors in his decision, he said, had been the proximity of Mont Saint-Michel. Upon hearing this, I went to fetch my half-read biography of Littré, and showed Yann a section which contained a quote about his childhood. Littré had been born in Paris, on the Rue des Grands-Augustins, but his father, Michel-François, had been born in Avranches, into a family of gold- and silversmiths that had lived there for generations. Littré wrote, in the preface to one of his books, about his father's hometown:

> I love Normandy, and I belong to Normandy. My father was born in Avranches. It's a small, isolated town, perched out on a kind of cape. But you must see the area when the apple trees are in blossom. It is bewitching, and as you gaze over its glory, you can also take in Mont Saint-Michel and its surrounding shoals without a single soul upon them. The effect of this ancient and much-lauded granite building, thrown into the ocean as though in defiance, is absolutely majestic. Twice a day the tide roars in, and the monastery is cut off from the world.

I'd visited Mont Saint-Michel more than ten years before. It was an incredibly cold day, even for winter, and I'd been on holiday in Brittany. On the way back, I stopped in Dinard and took a bus to the monastery. I was really tired and had fallen asleep, only to be woken by the excited voices of the other passengers. I looked out of the window, and there it was, at the end of the road which stretched out across the shoal: the centuries-old Gothic abbey of the Benedictine monks. I'd seen countless photos of Mont Saint-Michel and had read all sorts of articles about it, but its overwhelming mass as it soared into the sky took my breath away. At high tide, the water rushed in, surrounding the abbey and completely cutting it off from the mainland, making it look like an enormous rocky fortress emerging from the sea. The view of the abbey from Avranches, however, would be rather different from the south, which is what is usually in photographs. The distance might also mean that the abbey really would look about the size of something that had been "thrown" into the sea.

"That description sounds about right," Yann said. "In fact, Avranches is even further east than that village on the hill where we couldn't see anything from. Hey, what time is it now?"

"Seven-thirty."

"Then I think we can make it." Yann was already halfway up from his chair.

"Make what?"

"Mont Saint-Michel. We've got a while before the sun goes down. I'm hoping to take you to a secret spot that I know. Then we can eat something on the way back."

Without a moment's hesitation, I picked up the phone and called my hotel in Paris, telling them that I wouldn't be coming back that evening, and not to worry about me.

Then to Yann, I said, "All right. I'm ready to go with you wherever you take me."

Yann smiled, and suddenly he was in a really good mood.

In his truck, Yann floored it. The evening sky was brooding and unsettled, light showers suddenly pierced with rays of purple sun. The main road was pretty busy, as large delivery trucks that had made the trip from England on the ferry sped past. The drive was taking longer than I expected. Cars switched their headlights on, as the sky turned a light yellow, with layers of cloud and light forming what resembled a piecrust. We were running out of daylight, and if we wanted to get somewhere for a view, we'd have to get there fast. The signs said no overtaking, but Yann did so anyway, boldly pulling into the other lane whenever he had the chance. We turned on to a gravel road, which gradually got narrower and narrower, as we headed for the outskirts of Saint-Jean-le-Thomas. Eventually we cut across a piece of farmland with a white picket fence. A placard told us that we were on a private road.

"Is this OK? We're trespassing," I said.

"It's fine. I know the person who owns this land. Every summer teachers from the local high school bring students here to see the geological strata. They stay in that big house over there. I joined in one year after I got interested in geology while working at the stone factory. Exposed cliffs like these are the best for studying limestone. And don't worry, the light is OK. We're going to make it. Now, close your eyes for the next two minutes."

"Close my eyes? Why?"

"Just close them."

I did as I was told and closed my eyes. At times like these, Yann became a kind of hero who was in charge of everything. It was the same when he threw a winning pétanque—I could picture his face. The car went over a few bumps and dips in the road. With my eyes closed, I couldn't tell if we were driving straight ahead or taking a corner. Eventually the car stopped, and Yann turned off the engine. "Don't open your eyes until I tell you to," Yann said, as he got out of the driver's seat. He came round to my side, opened my door, then took my hand.

He led me up a gravel path that didn't feel very solid underfoot. There was a strong wind buffeting me too. Before long, I could hear the sound of waves, echoing from below, as they crashed against the shore.

"Open."

I opened my eyes to find Yann and me standing on a bluff, jutting out about thirty or forty metres above the sea below. There was no handrail, nothing, just a natural observation deck with spectacular views. The sea glittered in the evening sun, and we could see the tide moving in small waves, almost like crawling foam. To my right I had a clear sightline to the castle town of Saint Malo, fifteen kilometres away. To my left, at the bottom of the cliff, I could catch glimpses of old structures that had been built by the fishermen who lived here in ancient times. Further out, the sun was shining on the exposed sand, forming glowing yellow bands. Mont Saint-Michel was directly in front of us, seeming to float, enveloped in a pale, misty light. The abbey looked like a solitary chess piece that had been deployed in the water, and the vision of it from the side completely cleared away the stroppiness I'd been feeling from having my eyes closed. A fierce wind came up from below, blowing hard against me, my clothes and my hair rippling in the gust, almost taking my glasses away. It pushed me backwards, and as I inhaled, it blew straight up my nose and down my throat. I found myself struggling to breathe.

In the next second, the wind seemed to die down, and the view that Émile Littré had written of 150 years ago was laid out before me. The harmony between ocean and sky. The subtle changes in colour that permeated every nook and cranny of the wall of clouds. Everything seemed perfectly controlled. In the exposed section of the beach below, a fisherman was walking along slowly, examining his nets. He didn't seem to be in a hurry, so he might not have been checking his nets at all, just taking a walk, but every now and again he would bend down and touch the sand. When he did this, he looked like he could have been a bird. Over in the east, houses lined the coastal road that ran along the embankment. It didn't feel possible that just that morning I'd opened the window of my grimy one-star Paris hotel and looked down into an inner courtyard that was about as airy as the bottom of a well.

"This is my favourite place," Yann said.

I didn't say anything, didn't know what to say.

"Say something!" Yann shouted.

"It's amazing!" I shouted back.

"Anything else?"

"It makes me want to throw a Camembert as far as I can."

"A Camembert?"

He had been staring out to sea, but he now turned to face me, looking as though he were smiling through tears.

I pulled my right arm into my chest and crouched. Then mimicking a discus throw—slowly, so that I wouldn't tumble off the bluff—I launched my invisible cheese into the ocean at a 45-degree angle.

"53.28 metres!" I announced.

Yann was clearly amused, or bemused, but he stood silent, as though he had no words.

When we got back into the car and out of the wind, Yann turned to me and said, "You haven't changed at all! Only you would think of a Camembert in a place like that." He was shaking his head and laughing. I explained how the student on the train had told me about the Camembert discus throw and apologized for ruining his elaborate romantic choreography. Now we were both laughing.

Talking about Camembert made me realize I hadn't had anything but that little sandwich earlier in the afternoon. "Let's go to a restaurant," I said. "I'm starved, and my stomach is growling."

We drove to Avranches and looked around for a restaurant, but there were only pizza and crêpe places. I kept saying how that wouldn't really satisfy us, so we drove north, to the port town of Granville, where we turned off the main road and found ourselves at a quiet wharf, lined with touristy restaurants. We settled on one that seemed appealing and walked in. Most of the customers were elderly tourists, seemingly refined, apparently from across the channel. The two young waitresses shyly made their way among them, taking orders with their limited English. When our turn came, Yann ordered mussels and sautéed cod, holding off the wine because, as he said, he was responsible for driving me home. I ordered the same, opting for mineral water. The mussels didn't have much salt or wine in the broth, allowing for a nice, simple flavour. The cod, on the other hand, was dry and tasteless, and it was immediately obvious the fish had been frozen, even though we were right next to the sea. It was pretty disappointing.

"Well," Yann said, "at least we made it to Mont Saint-Michel in time, but it might have been more useful for your work if we'd gone to Avranches instead."

"No, no. It's been years since I went to Mont Saint-Michel, and that was via Pontorson so I experienced it in a totally different way. I really enjoyed it. Hey, do you remember that bit of Littré you read? Right after that there's an anecdote about the abbey at Mont Saint-Michel. I'll read it to you—better than me trying to summarize it."

I dug the book out of my bag, and began reading the passage to him in a low voice:

This is a story I have heard my family tell. One of my ancestors—he was a metalworker, just like his father and his children—was summoned to the abbey to undertake a complete restoration of a bronze sculpture that depicted the Archangel Michael triumphant over Satan. He was a conscientious man, my ancestor, so when he had finished examining the artwork, he gave his honest opinion to the Brothers. "Your devil's good, but the angel's worthless," he said. Unfortunately for

him, he was a Huguenot, and his words were miscon-
strued by the monks as a comment on their faith. My
ancestor became uneasy, and frightened, and in time
converted. My family have called themselves Catholic
ever since. What a reason to convert! If my ancestor
hadn't made his fateful remark, my family would still
be Huguenots, cursed forever.

Yann had listened to me with an utterly blank expression, massaging his temples with his thumbs. When I'd
stopped reading, he took the book from my hands and
started going through the passage again, slowly, silently,
seeming to be underlining it in his mind. Except for the
quiet conversation of the other customers, the restaurant
was quiet. I could hear ropes banging against boats in the
harbour, sounding as though some creature was ringing
a cluster of bells. Everything seemed to be on the same
wavelength as Yann read in silence, his earrings hanging
from his lobes and seeming to clink with the ringing of
the bells. I hadn't had anything to drink, but my brain felt
drunk. It was as if I were wearing heavy headphones, the
kind used in hearing tests, and there were an irregular,
almost imperceptible electronic tone coming through.

Yann now looked up at me. "Have you read *Literature
or Life* by Jorge Semprún?" he asked.

"No, I haven't read it, but I know about it." I was familiar with Semprún. He was best known for having survived
a couple of years in the Buchenwald concentration camp,
which was near the city of Weimar. Several of his novels

are about this period. *Literature or Life* was supposed to be the culmination of his work, and was a big best-seller, but there was something in-your-face about Semprún, and it put me off. "What's the connection to Littré?"

"Semprún was like most survivors of Buchenwald—he didn't want to ever see the place again. But forty-seven years after he left it, a German journalist invited him to visit the site, which had been preserved as a museum, and to be part of a TV programme about the mixed history of Weimar. After all, Goethe had lived there too. Semprún was interviewed in the camp itself, and the climax of the interview was this story he told about a 'fateful remark'. Up until that point, the programme didn't seem so interesting, but this part was intense.

"The story went like this: In 1987, Semprún for some reason had decided to awaken his memories of Buchenwald and write about his time there. He wrote in the first person, rather than from the perspective of a third person, looking from the outside in. But soon after he'd begun the book, he heard on the radio that Primo Levi, a fellow concentration camp survivor, had jumped to his death at his Turin flat, although there was the possibility that he had fallen accidentally. The news stunned him. Levi had been a model for Semprún, and his death contained a despair that undid everything. Semprún stopped writing. He did a stint as the Spanish Minister of Culture under González, and then, in 1992, he was given this completely unexpected chance to visit the concentration camp, which his book was to be about.

"Prisoners at Buchenwald were either dispatched to large factories that produced V-1 and V-2 rockets, or kept in the camp to maintain the place. If they were sent to factories, the labour conditions were so horrible that many never returned; it was like a death sentence. Semprún had been active in the French Resistance, got arrested in 1943 and was sent to Buchenwald in January 1944. Upon his arrival at the camp, the guard issuing registration cards asked Semprún what his occupation was. Semprún answered that he was a *student der philosophie*. The guard replied that *student* wasn't an occupation; if he wanted to survive in the camp, he needed to have a real trade, like electrician or plasterer. But Semprún was young and impudent and insisted that he was a student of philosophy, nothing else. The guard said OK and wrote *student* on the registration card. Years later, Semprún, who did indeed survive the camp, recounted this scene in one of his novels—as a heroic moment of defiance at the gates of hell.

"When he revisited Buchenwald, forty-seven years after the fact, to be interviewed by German TV, he shared this anecdote with the people at the museum. That was when a staff member, who was an avid reader of Semprún, piped up and said Semprún's account was incorrect. This staff member, in anticipation of Semprún's visit, had gone into the camp's archives and looked up the registration cards of prisoners who'd arrived in January 1944, and he had a copy of Semprún's card with him. What the guard had written down was not *student* but 'stuckateur'—plasterer! Semprún's attitude with the Buchenwald guard had convinced him that he had prevailed, and the fact that the first three letters of the two words were the same made it easy for him to think that was the case. But this was the fateful detail, for one month after Semprún arrived at Buchenwald, prisoners without utilitarian skills were transferred to a hard labour camp. So this one word on Semprún's registration card allowed him to remain in Buchenwald. It saved his life.

"It's a bad joke if life hangs on what's written in the 'occupation' box on a prisoner's registration card. It's the same with the angel and the devil. Who's to know what was the 'right' thing? If Littré's family had stayed Huguenot, they'd have been oppressed during the religious wars, and would have had to live through a really tough history. It's not like because they were Catholic they were safe, but they definitely were on a safer path, and it was all because of that stupid remark. The same with Semprún. There's nothing stupid about saying you're a plasterer, of course. But in the end, what the guard deliberately wrote on that card saved his life, and that's pretty ironic. And Littré's ancestor knew how to work with metals, right? He wasn't a religious devotee or anything. Maybe that's why they let him get away with it?"

I caught the attention of the waitress and ordered us two coffees. The conversation had gone off on an unexpected tangent, and as Yann was talking, I suddenly remembered something that had happened soon after we'd become friends—on the same day we went to the

Jewish deli together, in fact. Thinking about it now, I'd probably imagined it was symbolic.

"Do you remember when Bettelheim killed himself?" I asked.

"Yeah, I was just thinking about that while I was speaking."

It had been shortly before I moved out of my shared apartment, so in 1990, maybe early spring. I'd woken in the morning, switched on the radio and heard that the great child psychologist Bruno Bettelheim had killed himself in a senior citizens' home in Chicago. He was eighty-six, and had been a survivor of Buchenwald too. Yann had studied child psychology and communication theory before getting a science degree and had occasionally mentioned Bettelheim's name, so I called him immediately to let him know. He'd been listening to the same news bulletin, and kept saying he couldn't believe Bettelheim had killed himself. Bettelheim's theories were pretty heavy-handed, and there were many things I couldn't agree with, but the larger body of his work had a power that transcended simple psychology. And when he wrote about treating children with autism, he often reflected upon his experience in the concentration camps.

Yann's reaction to Bettelheim's suicide hadn't been what I expected: "Even if you're really scared of getting old, how can a person like that kill themselves at this stage in life? I don't understand it. First Levi, now Bettelheim, what's going on?" He wasn't grieving the loss of someone. He was lamenting their failures.

"Talking about Littré got us to a weird place," I said as the coffee arrived.

"Sorry about that. Meeting again after all these years, I should be talking about something more cheerful."

"I don't feel that way at all. It was good. Anyway, since you've got to pack for tomorrow, why don't we leave here and continue the conversation at your place? This meal is on me."

"You mean you're going to pay? Now that really is stupid... This is on me."

"No, it's fine. I was the one who made a fuss about being hungry. And besides, I've got a favour to ask."

"What's that?"

I pointed at the porcelain dish in which the butter had come to the table. It was white, with the curious name of the local manufacturer, Elle & Vire, printed in blue. It didn't have a lid and was probably mass-produced.

"It's not anything special, but I want to take it home with me as a memento of this trip. I'm too embarrassed to ask, but could you?"

"Sure, though it's not really a fair deal for your listening to all that heavy stuff."

Yann asked for the bill, and explained my request to the waitress. I paid by credit card, wrapped the butter dish up in a napkin and stuffed it in my rucksack. As we made our way back to the truck, the ropes continued to clank against the hulls of the boats in the harbour.

Yann had the radio on as we drove back, and he rapped along with a song I didn't know, moving his upper body in

cut in it; a stone apple-press for making cider; a sixteen-wheel truck, stuck in stationary traffic on the highway. These were Yann's photos all right, there was no doubt about that. There were also photos of people: Armenian twin girls he'd met at a dance studio in Avranches; an old woman, wrapped in a thick shawl, sitting in silence on a bench; a homeless person lying next to some driftwood on the beach. I was impressed, and I asked if I could have one to take home with me, one that he'd be willing to part with. He started leafing through a box that hadn't been sorted, and finally pulled out a photo of a wooden shed—with a façade of horizontal planks and four small, evenly spaced windows. At the base of the structure, on the grass, was a three-layer shelf made from crude pieces of scrap lumber, on which sat rows of pipe joints of various sizes, each in the shape of a curled index finger. The pipes were weather-beaten, their surfaces were corroding, and their openings all pointed in the same direction, making them resemble tired men lining up in military formation. In the foreground of the photo was stretched some barbed wire that looked brand-new.

"See how the windows are different? Do you know what this building is for?"

It wasn't a fisherman's hut, and it wasn't a barn. There was something austere about it, but it had a kind of geometrical elegance too. I wouldn't have been surprised if it had been a science lab.

"A cider mill?"

"You're on the right track, but no."

"A place for quarry workers to take a break?"

"Nope. It's a place for smoking pork."

I'd never seen a smokehouse before, so the mystery escaped me.

"When I took this photo, I thought it would be interesting. I didn't think about anything in particular beyond that. But then, when I saw the print, I suddenly got an uncomfortable feeling. I mean, look at these pipes. See over there, on the left? There's a black one that's longer than the others, right? That's the father. The head of the family. The pipe on the right, the bendy white one that's propped up on the top shelf, that's the mother. The rest are their kids. There's sixteen of them, total. Sixteen. That's how many were in my grandmother's family."

"What do you mean?"

I looked up, but Yann's eyes were focused elsewhere.

"Those four small windows," he went on, "you don't push and pull them open and shut—you raise and lower them. They're just like windows in isolation cells."

"Like in a concentration camp? You mean this reminded you of a concentration camp?"

"Yeah."

"Like these pipes would be used to pump in gas? Or they'd use this place as a crematorium?"

"Well... I guess that's possible. But the reason I imagined something so absurd was the barbed wire. Can you imagine, I didn't even notice it until the photo was developed? Anyway, it's yours now. I don't want to throw it away, and I don't want to keep it. I guess the roles are reversed, and now I'm asking you a favour. Take it with you, OK?"

"When was it taken?"

"Quite recently. I happened on the place while I was driving around."

"But old houses and ruined workshops, stuff like that, they're a theme of your work, right? So, in that sense alone, I'd say it's an interesting photo. Maybe you're overthinking this. Maybe it's because of reading Semprún?"

Yann got up and went over to the stove. He put the kettle on to boil and then, without saying a word, headed upstairs. He came back down with a large picture frame, which he handed to me, then proceeded to make coffee in an old aluminium drip pot. In the frame was a family photograph, with several people surrounding an old woman seated in the middle. Was she Yann's grandmother? Everyone had very similar facial features, and it occurred to me that the old woman's face was the prototype for Yann's.

"That's my grandmother," Yann said, leaning over me. "She died before I moved here. You know, you say I'm overthinking things, and that's probably true. It's just that I have been wondering a lot lately about the education I received. Not at school, obviously. The education I got at home."

As he spoke, Yann poured coffee into the same chipped bowls we'd had our tea in that afternoon. The coffee from Catherine was supermarket coffee, from Beaumont, a large chain, and it smelled stale. Still, I had no right to complain about something that had been gifted to me and that I'd received with a bow.

"Do you remember when we went to Saint-Paul together?" Yann asked, picking up the thread of the conversation. "There's a Yiddish library in that area that my grandmother would go to sometimes—to read the newspaper, borrow books, talk to folks in Yiddish. But Yiddish wasn't spoken in my house. My parents knew it, and when I was a kid and relatives would come and visit us, they'd all speak this language that was completely foreign to me. I guess Yiddish was already beginning to die out. And now, the time when Jews from wherever they're from could communicate in Yiddish is long gone. The traditions still exist, of course. They're deep-rooted. We celebrate all the holidays and stuff. But the Yiddish language—my parents didn't teach it to my brother and me. Or maybe it's more correct to say, they didn't force it on us. They didn't try to pass it on to us. It seemed my grandmother was fine with that too. She never spoke about the past. My mother told me some stories of when she was a little girl, but that's all."

It was now pitch black outside, and there was no noise at all. Not the sound of the wind, or the sound of insects, or the sound of cars that would be ever present in the city. Yann didn't have a TV, we hadn't put on any music, and the only sounds to be heard were the coffee being drunk and our chairs creaking as we shifted in them. I picked up two lumps of sugar from a blue cardboard box and mindlessly dropped them in my coffee, even though I usually drink it without. I stirred the coffee, and the clinking of the spoon against porcelain was startling.

"There's a difference between the generation that knew the camps and the generation that doesn't," Yann went on. "A definite difference. Why didn't my parents teach me anything? It's strange, isn't it? When I asked them why, they said they didn't know the details. But my grand-mother received a pension from the German government until the day she died. An indemnity, I guess you could call it. It was enough to get by on, and she used the money to live out her later years. That alone had to be enough to keep her from escaping her memories. She also never stopped speaking Yiddish, or Polish, to my grandfather."

"You know, I still remember the carrot cake we had at your studio. You made it from your grandmother's recipe."

"Did we do that?"

"We definitely did."

"Yeah, I think I remember, now that you mention it. Anyway, what I always wanted to know was what their lives were like when they lived in Poland. She wouldn't talk about it, though. I never heard anything about what happened there, how they used to live, tales from their childhood. Nothing. Sure, I know their story isn't unusual—there are families with similar stories all over Europe.

"I mean, think about it: sixteen people in my grand-mother's family, and only four of them survived the war. You wonder if she had some magic word like 'plasterer' that allowed her to live. She was a pâtissière, so I guess she could bake bread. People need bread, even in a concentration camp." Yann now paused for a moment, then turned to face me. "Look, this isn't about righteous indignation, or crimes against humanity or anything like that. It's just that seeing the photo of the smoking hut made me sad, that's all, on a totally personal level. Maybe 'sad' isn't the right word."

Personal sadness. Was there any other kind? Wasn't sadness something that everyone had to endure individually? Just like anger. The idea that you can share anger or sadness with others is nothing more, really, than a compelling illusion. We can only communicate the pain we feel on an individual level. Maybe one reason Yann had an awkward relationship with his parents was less their silence about the past, and more their inability to understand the nature of Yann's sadness. He had often complained that neither his father nor his mother had ever tried to get out, to leave their town and go somewhere else. That might be why they didn't understand why he was always on the move and never went to visit them.

"The Wandering Jew is a cliché," Yann continued, "but there's a reason for it. Why shut yourselves in? Why hide away and close the door, pretending that the outside world doesn't exist? That's why I don't understand about Anne Frank. Well, about her father. The war wasn't imaginary, they needed to flee. They had lots of chances to do that, but they didn't. 'No, this is our home,' they thought, 'we're staying.' If I wanted to be cold about it, I could say they had a chance to escape and they missed it."

I was unclear why that one photo of the smokehouse had fired up Yann so much. Was he being dramatic—like he used to be in his twenties? Was he was getting high off the sound of his own voice? No, his words were forceful, but his demeanour was quite calm.

Yann went on: "I saw something similar in Bosnia. The news was all about people being killed, persecuted, beaten, raped, forced to work... I wanted to see the situation with my own eyes. I should say that this was before I read Semprún. A charity based in Avranches arranged for me and a girl who spoke the language to go to a town that had been bombed in the war to do some reporting. I didn't take my camera, though. I didn't think photographing it would make any difference. I just wanted to witness it. The area we went to was on the border, which was marked by a river. The local kids used to come and go over the bridge merrily, but then overnight people on one side of the river became enemies of people on the other side. Kids were shot just for crossing the river to play. One day we encountered a family on the move—they'd had to flee a bombardment. I had the interpreter ask where they were going, and they said they were going back. Can you believe that? Going back to their bombed-out house. They let us go with them, and they took us to an apartment block that had been reduced to rubble. I asked why they wanted to come back here, and they said, 'This is our home.' The same thing that had happened to my family during the Second World War was happening here. I felt dizzy. It was exactly the same thing, happening again."

I got up and went to the toilet. I wasn't sure how to respond and thought it best to change the subject. When I returned to the room, I picked up some photos from the table, thumbed through them, laid them back down. In the limited reality that I knew, I'd never had to flee for my life, and it was unlikely to happen now. If I went somewhere, I always returned. I left Paris and came to this village; soon enough I would go back to Paris, then I would go back to Tokyo. But in a way I was always at home. If you were to make a contact sheet of all my journeys, and looked at them retrospectively, it would be clear that all my travels were return trips, and that I never drifted anywhere. In that sense, Yann and I were different. Even though there's something about us that's connected, we're moving in different directions, and we're never going to collide. Maybe the shell fire I sought out was a different species from his.

"Welcome to chez Yann," I suddenly said boldly.

"What?"

"Welcome to chez Yann. That's what you said, when we first got here this afternoon and you showed me in. You looked really happy too. I know that it was a big step for you to move here from Paris, but you didn't tell your father that you were living here, did you? You told him you'd 'put down anchor'. You don't welcome people to your house like that if you're just putting down anchor, though."

"I guess so."

There was an awkward silence. I picked up the photos again. There were several shots of the doors of old buildings—some houses, some sheds—made of planks of coarse wood. Individually, they looked rather ordinary, each with a square opening to let the light in. Viewed one after another, however, they started to form an uncanny rhythm with all the differences in size and shape. There were also shots of a corner of a barn filled with pulleys and ladders, a kitten staring at a chicken, a dog closing its eyes as it basked in the sun, a crumbling pillbox of the sort that were still to be found on the coast of Normandy. Yann was focusing on my fingers as I silently leafed through the photos. A waiter in a cafe sweeping the floor, all the chairs stacked up on tables; three fat girls buying crêpes; a pure white cow's head in a butcher shop window... It slowly occurred to me that the photo of the smokehouse, which had reminded Yann of a concentration camp, was bothering me. I didn't think I could accept it and I didn't think I could refuse it, so I guess I was going through the other pictures half intending to see if I could find one I could take instead. I came across a series of photographs of a play that had been staged outdoors at night. In one, a middle-aged woman was crouching down in the middle of the stage, and a man in a suit was embracing her. A spotlight was on them.

"Those photos are of a drama festival celebrating the fiftieth anniversary of the Normandy landings. It was staged in the square in Avranches—your favourite place."

"It's not my favourite place at all. I haven't even had a chance to look around it yet."

"Right. Well, anyway, the Avranches town council commissioned this particular play, asking that it be set in the town itself. The playwright interviewed lots of people, people who'd lived in Avranches for years, and wrote his play based on the stories they told him. It's weird that you'd pick that one photo out of the bunch, though."

"Why's that?"

"Because, like it or not, it's connected to what we were talking about before. The main subject of the play was a Jewish family who lived in Avranches. The young wife had just given birth to a baby. Knowing that it was a matter of time before the Gestapo came for them, she sneaked off to the neighbouring village and gave the baby to a farm family there. You remember Saint-Jean-le-Thomas, that nice place we went through today? That's where she took her baby. The farm family was surprised, and scared. Even if the kid wasn't Jewish, if the Germans found out they were hiding a baby, they'd be done for.

"But the farm family understood the situation, and they were brave. They raised the infant girl as if she were their own. They named her Estelle. In the play, the scene where Estelle's mother pleads with the farm family to take her daughter is the climax—a really powerful moment for the choice she makes and all the risks involved. The mother and her husband go down a path that leads to their death, while their daughter is raised, in safety, by people who have no blood relation to her.

"On the night the play was staged, Estelle, the actual daughter who was now middle-aged, was invited to see the performance from the front row of the outdoor theatre. She knew her history: her adoptive parents had told her.

She knew the risks her birth mother took in saving her, and the courage of her adoptive parents in raising her. Despite all this, it was an inescapable fact that she did not know what her birth mother looked like or sounded like. That night in the theatre, it was as if Estelle was meeting her mother for the first time. At curtain call, the director invited Estelle up to the stage, announcing that the play had been written and performed for her. Estelle came to the stage, but sort of collapsed. She couldn't stand up, she could barely speak. For Estelle, the actress playing her mother was her real mother. The baby who had been born in the year of the Normandy landings and who was now in middle age broke down in tears in the director's arms."

Yann had only been at the play by chance, because his friend was involved with the production, and had been at a loss for words as he clicked his shutter.

Yann considered his family's history and its unsuccessful transmission from generation to generation as something quite "ordinary", and neither disregarded it nor ignored it. This was probably because he had lived his life in a place where the pain of such tragedies continued to affect the people around him. For me, though, it wasn't "ordinary", and I didn't want to own a photograph like that, its focus revealing the fact that the photographer had been deeply moved. Yann's story was enough for me. And anyway, what I wanted right then was a quieter image, one enveloped in a softer glow. Sure, Yann had chosen the first photo for me, but the fact that I'd followed up a photo that reminded him of a concentration camp with a photo that had to do with the Gestapo just didn't seem like it could have been a coincidence. I wanted a different darkness as well as a different light, something to clear away that heavy stone weight.

I picked up the bunch of photographs again, and eventually pulled out a snapshot-like photo of an adorable baby, about a year old. He was sleeping peacefully, his large eyes closed, lying on a sofa with a soft woollen cover that looked hand-knitted. Even though it's such a cliché that I'd hesitate to say it in my native tongue, the baby really did look angelic. And he seemed happy. I thought—oddly, to be sure—of the glossy cheeks of a baby born by Caesarean section; one who had not passed through the birth canal, who was unblemished by natural birth. The baby's skin seemed so soft as to be not of this world, and though I knew nothing of how lighting is technically achieved, its body also seemed to be illuminated by a warmth that made me feel at ease. The baby had an expression which did not yet know the complexities of destiny—enemies, allies and life.

"I like his face," I said. "His forehead is incredible. Especially in that filtered light you've got on the sofa."

"Yeah, I know. He can't appreciate any of that, though."

"What?"

"He can't see anything, he's blind. He's Catherine's son, you know."

"This is Catherine's son?"

"Yes. His name's David. Actually, when I say he's blind, it's not just that he can't see. He doesn't have any eyeballs.

It's a hereditary condition. So he'd be totally oblivious to that light you were just praising."

I looked again at the photograph. David was leaning against a large stuffed teddy bear. I stared at his thick eyelashes. His eye sockets did not look especially hollow, and I wouldn't have guessed that he was blind if Yann hadn't told me.

"Can he hear?"

"His ears are perfect, no problems at all. This photo was taken over a year ago, he's grown a fair bit since then. Catherine teaches everything to him with words. 'This is water, these are clothes, this is your teddy bear.' Maybe she uses words to describe the light too."

David was Catherine's first child, born ten years after she and her husband were married. Yann had initially met the husband through work, and this was how he'd come to rent the house. In the beginning Catherine was quite reserved around Yann, maybe because of the marital problems she was having, and so they'd had a strictly tenant–landlord relationship. Things had gradually started to change after David was born and Catherine and her husband decided to split up, but it was only quite recently that she and Yann had become close. The teddy bear David was leaning on had been made by Catherine herself. She'd started creating it as soon as she found out she was pregnant, even though she hadn't done anything like that before, and indeed it was obvious from the photograph that the bear was not store-bought. Still, there was no question of anyone failing to recognize it as a bear, and it had a simple functionality about it. In the months before the photo had been taken, it seemed the bear had become rather like a pet, an animal that had grown fond of David and allowed its similarly-sized master to rest his head on its shoulder.

The more I looked at the photo, which had such a tranquillity to it, something didn't feel right, and a weight, a tiny discordance, lodged itself in my chest.

"I hate to tell you this, since it seems you're really into it, but don't get attached to that photo," Yann said, interrupting my momentary reverie. "I don't have a negative for it, and I'm not giving it to you." That was when I realized the thing bothering me, and an involuntary "uh" escaped from my mouth: the bear's eyes had been stitched over in the shape of an x. It had a nose and a mouth, but its eyes had been sewn shut. Those sewn-shut eyes meant that the bear was looking after David at the same time as the bear was being looked after by David—which made their relationship considerably more complex. In fact, as I kept looking at it, I found it impossible to say whether the bear was laughing or crying or anything.

"So the teddy bear's got—"

"No eyes," Yann finished the sentence for me. "It did when Catherine first made it. Big black buttons, borrowed from an old coat. Catherine finished the bear before David was born. Then she learned that he was blind and she got rid of the buttons and stitched the eyes shut."

"To make it more like her son?"

day he died. In the end, it seemed that Émile Littré's parents were both agreed that the education of their child was more important than religion.

Michel-François was transferred to Angoulême, and took his young family with him. He and his wife had two more children, a girl and a boy, but when Émile was ten years old, the girl died of an illness, which devastated Émile. The family returned to Paris and settled in what is now known as the Rue Champollion. Michel-François, who had been a passionate scholar with a strong interest in languages, even going so far as learning Sanskrit, would hold Thursday study sessions for his son and his friends, and it soon became apparent that Émile had an aptitude for linguistics. Émile entered the Lycée Louis-le-Grand, where he was in the same year as Louis Hachette, who would go on to establish one of France's largest publishing houses and who would be instrumental in the publication of Littré's famous dictionary.

After graduating from the Lycée at the age of eighteen, Émile felt that his scientific knowledge was lacking, and with the goal of gaining admission to a highly regarded school of science and technology, he embarked on studies in mathematics. No amount of effort was enough, however, and so he started searching for a means to support himself. He worked as a private secretary for the statesman Pierre Daru, but this did not last long. In fact, it was Daru himself who told Littré that he might do better taking another path. Despite his fascination with science, Littré was resistant to the treatment of human problems as abstractions. And with the limits to his mathematical ability, Littré now felt that the only path open to him was medicine.

With his father's blessing, he matriculated at the medical school of the University of Paris, where he diligently applied himself to his studies for seven years, under the tutelage of Pierre François Olive Rayer—a pioneer in the field of nephrology. When Littré was twenty-seven, his father, on whom he had been financially dependent, died suddenly. His medical intern's salary was insufficient to support his mother and brother, so in order to earn additional money, he started submitting articles to a recently launched medical magazine. This led to his being offered a job as an editor, and eventually he was assigned the task of translating the complete works of Hippocrates. He quit his job as an intern, abandoning his medical career when all he needed for his degree was to submit a final thesis. Littré declared that he was quitting for financial reasons, but he rejected all his friends' offers of help. Instead he took a post at the *Le National* newspaper, which was edited by Armand Carrel, a shrewd operator and an avowed opponent of King Louis-Philippe. Littré spent several years translating articles from English and German for the newspaper until one day Carrel, during a spell in prison, happened to read an article Littré had written. Carrel was very impressed, and as soon as he was released, gave Littré an official position as a columnist. Despite his new job, Littré maintained a friendship with his old mentor Rayer and an interest in the medical field, and in 1832 he published a paper on cholera. Two years later, in the pages of *Le National*, he published a detailed analysis on the transmission of the disease. It was well received and was later considered to be a pioneering piece of what would go on to be called sociology—the discipline developed by Auguste Comte, whom Littré greatly admired. In 1836, Littré's great champion Carrel died at the age of thirty-six, shot in a duel with Émile de Girardin, the self-styled newspaper king and founder of *La Presse*, which carried serialized novels and featured groundbreaking page layouts.

Littré continued to work and in 1839 published the first volume of his translation of the complete works of Hippocrates. The tenth and final volume was completed in 1861. While devoting time to this translation and its annotation, Littré developed a deep interest in the origin of French words, and in 1841 he revealed his idea for the "Dictionnaire étymologique de la langue française" to his close friend Louis Hachette. Hachette's reaction was favourable, and he even paid Littré an advance so that he could start working on it immediately. But Littré's attentions were divided: his beloved mother died around then, and he needed to complete his translation of Hippocrates. Five years passed, and he had barely made a start on the dictionary. Hachette became exasperated, and tore up their old contract. He then encouraged his friend to create a type of dictionary that had never been seen before—one that not only contained the etymologies and definitions, but also provided examples of contemporary usage. Littré hesitated. His main interest was in investigating and describing the etymology of words. That alone was an enormous task, and now Hachette was pushing him to compile a dictionary that included examples of modern usage as well. In the end, he accepted the challenge. The *Dictionnaire de l'Académie française*, which he used for reference, did not contain technological or scientific terms, and had no quotations featuring words as they were used. Littré therefore set about compiling a list of new words in fields that were suitable for the nineteenth century. He looked through texts dating from the distant past to the present day and, with the help of his assistants, read and reread extracts from pre-eminent writers, writing sample sentences on cards. Littré devoted himself to the work despite numerous new interruptions: the sudden death, in July 1864, of Louis Hachette, who had been waiting patiently for Littré to finish his dictionary; a year spent writing a biography of August Comte, after Comte's widow's begged him to; the outbreak of the Franco-Prussian War; the chaos of the Paris Commune. Eventually, his dictionary was published in four volumes; the first one in 1863, and the fourth and final in 1873. It had taken over thirty years for it to reach fruition. The dictionary exceeded everyone's wildest expectations, and was reprinted many times. After it was published, Littré, who by now had served as a member of Parliament, was elected to be a member of the Académie française. In 1875 he became a senator, his reputation as a literary figure well and truly established. He continued to work on his dictionary, making revisions and additions for future printings, until his death in June 1881. All this meant that Émile Littré, a man who had achieved much in his life and made significant contributions to his country, would a century later become a figure of caricature—his countenance, with those big bullfrog lips, rejected by high school students for its ugliness.

I CLOSED MY BOOK.

Littré had lived in Le Mesnil-le-Roi in the Seine-et-Oise department. His house was old and small, though it did have a sizeable garden. He would arise at eight each morning and, while his wife was tidying his bedroom-cum-study, would go downstairs and work on such simple tasks as writing a preface. Then, at nine o'clock, he'd go back upstairs and pick up the proofs of his dictionary. After he'd finished lunch, at one o'clock, he'd return to his desk and work on articles for the *Journal des savants* until three. Between three and six, he'd immerse himself in his dictionary once again. He'd also work on the dictionary, after dinner, between seven and midnight. His wife and daughter would then go to bed, while Littré would continue working until three in the morning. Though there may have been minor distractions, Littré faithfully repeated this schedule every day for over a decade. It must have required an astounding level of physical, let alone mental, tenacity and spiritual strength.

Here I was in Normandy, reading about Littré's life in a house much like his, and I was exhausted after just one day. I had no means of diversion or entertainment, so I just lay on the sofa, smoking and staring at the photo Yann had given me.

The photo I'd eventually decided on was of the granite factory, a shot that Yann himself acknowledged had come out well. There was the factory building, which had a corrugated iron roof, and on the ground in front of it was a pile of cubic stones, just tossed there, as if discarded. Overhead, the sky was filled with an ominous cloud, which made rain seem imminent. The stones of the wall of the factory were all different sizes and shapes, a little bit higgledy-piggledy. In stark contrast, the exposed ends of the stones in the pile seemed all cleanly cut. In fact, it was this contrast between the two that made it an interesting composition.

As I gazed at that mound of stones, mindlessly piled together, one random thought led to another, and I had the sudden urge to see how Littré had defined a paving stone. Yann had said he had some volumes of Littré's dictionary. There was no bookshelf in the downstairs living room, though, so I supposed they had to be upstairs. I hadn't thought of going up there since that was Yann's private space, but I decided to make an exception for Littré. I climbed the ancient stairs, each one creaking as I made my way up.

The loft was bigger than I had imagined. The area where Yann had his bed was separated from the area where he had his desk by a large, wall-like bookcase that was filled with boxes of negatives, magazines and an array of books. There was a row of A.E. van Vogt novels, which I remembered from Yann's apartment in Paris. Beneath them, on the bottom shelf, were the heavy dictionaries I was looking for. And just as he claimed, there was the partial set of the Littré—two volumes of a reissued edition from the 1950s. He had Volume 1, which contained Littré's 1880 essay "How I Came to Create a French Dictionary". The other volume, by sheer chance, included the words beginning with P. Flicking rapidly through the musty pages, I found what I was looking for—"*pavé*". A masculine noun. "Block of sandstone or hard stone, used for road surfacing". The definition was so straightforward, I almost felt betrayed. But then my eyes were drawn to the first example of usage that he'd given. It was a quote from La Fontaine: *The loyal fly-chaser picked up a paving stone, and threw it as hard as it could.*

Huh? What kind of situation would cause someone deliberately to throw a heavy paving stone at a fly? Who would even think to do a thing like that? I was not very familiar with La Fontaine, so it didn't ring any bells, though I suspected anyone who'd had their early education in France might have got it straight away. If Yann were here, he probably could have given me a hint. Unfortunately, the only way I was going to figure it out was to read La Fontaine's *Fables*—Book 8, Fable 10—Littré had been thorough enough to indicate where the quote had come from. I had a quick rummage through the rows of paperbacks on Yann's bookshelves, but there weren't any old classics. My inability to find the fable only fuelled my urge to get a hold of it. Maybe there'd be some La Fontaine at a bookshop in Avranches. I'd look for it while I waited for my train back to Paris.

Until a short while ago, I'd felt very comfortable in Yann's house, but now I couldn't wait to leave, all because of a couple of little words. This felt quite fickle, even by my standards, but I couldn't help it. That very strange combination of "fly" and "paving stone" had seized me. Yann's bed looked inviting, but I ignored it and went back downstairs. I lay down on the sofa, which was familiar territory, and fell into a deep sleep.

The next morning, after I'd had some coffee and a walk to wake up, I dialled the number for Catherine that Yann had left for me. The phone rang for a long time before a husky voice answered.

"Is this Catherine?"

I realized that I'd neglected to learn her surname earlier, and I got flustered as I found myself forced to call her by her first name.

"Who's this?"

"I'm Yann's friend from Japan. We visited you a couple of days ago."

"Oh! Yes, hello there. I'm sorry I wasn't much of a host when you came round. Yann's already left, hasn't he?"

"Yes, we ended up not leaving together. I was thinking about going back to Paris today. Do you think you would be able to take me to the station, if it's convenient?"

"Of course. There is one condition, though."

"A condition?"

"You must come here for lunch first. After all, you don't have any food over there, do you?"

True, I did not have any food. "I'd be very happy to come over for lunch," I said.

"Good, I'll come and pick you up about twelve thirty then. Did Yann give you a key?"

"No, he told me I didn't need to lock up."

"Really? Well, I suppose it's just like him to go abroad without locking his front door... Just make sure the windows are closed then, to stop the rain getting in."

After hanging up, I washed the dishes in the sink, wiped the bathroom tiles, cleared the table I was working at, and made sure that everything in the house looked decent. Then I napped on the sofa for about an hour. Catherine came a little earlier than she said she would. I heard the car coming from far away, just like she must have heard us the other day, and I was outside waiting for her when she drove around the barn towards me. A little boy was in the passenger seat, holding a teddy bear. There wasn't anything of the baby from the photograph about him any more. He had thick blond hair flowing out from under his little cap and down to the nape of his neck. Catherine and I exchanged greetings.

"You're David, right? Hello." I took the boy's hand.

"Bonjour," David said, and smiled.

"How old is he?" I asked Catherine.

"He's nearly two and a half."

Of course, I couldn't say "It must be tough", or anything like that, but Catherine must have known that I was aware of the situation. I knew David's name, which meant Yann had told me about him. I had climbed into the back seat and was straddling the bump in the middle, meaning I could glance back and forth between Catherine and her son. David had grown big enough to hold his teddy bear in one hand. He called it Nounours, and sounded very cheerful. He seemed to be in a good mood.

After a bit, Catherine said, "Yann has told me about you, actually."

"Really?"

"I don't remember when it was. He told me he had a Japanese friend who was good at idling his days away, doing nothing. He seemed proud of it. Just because the stereotype was that Japanese people were all worker bees, it didn't mean there weren't exceptions, he said. He never did give me a name, but I guess he must have been talking about you, right?"

"I guess so. I don't think he knows that many idle Japanese people. Did you know that we met at a pétanque tournament?"

"Pétanque? Japanese people play pétanque?"

"Well, I just like throwing things. Camemberts, for example."

"Camembert? The cheese? Hah!" Catherine laughed, and looked at me in the rear-view mirror.

"Iron balls, Camembert cheeses... I'll throw anything as long as it's round," I said, and somehow thought about the La Fontaine character who threw the paving stone.

"You need a lot of free time to play pétanque, though. What were you doing then?"

"I was a student. Free time was the one thing I had plenty of."

"Yes, of course. You know, as soon as I met you the other night I knew you were the friend Yann had told me about."

"You could see me idling, even in the dark?"

"I thought I could," she said, laughing again. "I'm starting to see why you get along so well with Yann."

I didn't have a response. As though to compensate for that, David started tossing his teddy bear in the air and making happy noises. I could see the bear's eyes sewn shut with two crosses of red thread.

Catherine's house seemed completely different by daylight. It was a well-built stone structure, all on one floor and clinging fast to a sloping piece of land, so that it seemed to be ever so slightly out of kilter. Catherine showed me to the living room, which was just off the entrance hall, and asked me to relax there while she prepared the food. The room was quite large, with old exposed beams and a wooden floor. One corner seemed to be a play area, centred around a playpen. David plonked himself down on a cushion, and started to play happily, shaking a toy that had bells on it and chewing on some building blocks. The bear sat next to him in silence.

Catherine shouted from the kitchen if I minded the meat rare. I shouted back that that was fine, and wandered over to a heavy antique bookcase. My eyes immediately fell on a series of volumes with distinctive red lettering along their spines. I couldn't believe it—La Fontaine's *Fables*. The smell of garlic tickled my nostrils, and as I watched David playing out of the corner of my eye, I reached for Book 8 and flipped the pages to Fable 10. With the book in hand, I sat on the sofa next to David's playpen. The fable was called "The Bear and the Amateur Gardener"—La Fontaine always was fond of a crazy title.

Deep in the mountains, in a place that was barely accessible for animals and out of the question for humans, a bear lived all alone. Though bears are solitary creatures, even they eventually grow tired of being isolated, and of having no one to talk to. As luck would have it, an elderly amateur gardener lived not too great a distance away, and he too had grown to dislike his life, filled as it was with flowers but no conversation. He wanted a friend, and so he ventured out in search of one. Soon enough, he happened to come across the bear, which had come down from the mountains with the same goal in mind. The man was scared of the bear, of course, but he invited it to his house nonetheless, and cooked it dinner. They soon discovered that they were kindred spirits, and decided to live together. The bear would go out hunting, while the man worked diligently in the garden. The bear's most important job, however, was to chase pesky flies away from the man while he enjoyed his afternoon nap. One day, while the man was sleeping soundly, a fly came and landed on his nose. Try as he might, the bear could not chase it away. Determined to get rid of the fly no matter what, the loyal fly-chaser picked up a paving stone, and threw it as hard as it could, crushing the fly, of course, but also its friend's head.

Thus, the bear, who possessed few powers of reasoning but was capable of a mighty throw, killed the man as he slept. There is nothing more dangerous than a stupid friend. A wise enemy is far better.

The expression *le pavé de l'ours*, an unwanted intervention, has its origins in this cautionary tale, and was still in use. But leaving aside the tale's moral teachings, how on earth did a seventeenth-century poet come up with this gory scenario, one in which a bear throws a heavy paving stone to try and kill the fly, and succeeds only in splitting open his companion's skull? OK, so the lonely bear happened to meet the old man, but that alone did not seal their fate. For one thing, there would probably not have been a paving stone around had the man not been such a keen gardener. What's more, had he befriended almost any animal other than a bear, it wouldn't have been able to lift the paving stone to throw it at him. And what about the little fly that came between them? It would certainly have flown off at some point if they'd just let it be, and if the brawny bear really had to throw something at it, a

Camembert would have been much better. The fly would have liked the smell of the cheese, and even if it had hit the man in the head, it probably wouldn't have injured him badly. Mind you, if the bear hadn't thrown the stone, and had tried to swat the fly away with its powerful paws instead, the old man would probably have suffered the same grisly fate.

For a while, the terrible lengths which the fable went to in order to denounce unwanted interventions dulled my awareness of its conclusion—that there was nothing more dangerous than a foolish friend. It got me to wondering whether I was Yann's equivalent of La Fontaine's bear. There was "something about me" which made him talk about things he didn't need to talk about, made him expose his wounds. That surely made me more dangerous than a stranger who was totally indifferent. Still, I hoped that our shell fires still burned for each other. Yann had once told me a fable that was somewhat similar, so I don't think my existence bothered him or made him uncomfortable. But when I looked back at the kind of conversations we had, we spent more time on topics that mattered to us deeply than we did on ordinary day-to-day events. Of course, I couldn't deny that my limited facility at conversation was related to that. When we first were getting to know each other, Yann would try to condense what he was saying to the basic essence, omitting any modifiers. It would be wrong, though, simply to say that this became a habit—that this was why we jumped from one big issue to the next when we talked. Words and ideas seemed to flow from us naturally. Émile Littré and Jorge Semprún became connected in some abstract way—an illusion not unlike when the tide goes out at Mont Saint-Michel and the shoals which are revealed give the impression that one could walk along them forever. In much the same way, the jump now was from Littré's dictionary to La Fontaine's fable. Actually, though, maybe we were swatting at flies on each other that neither of us could see. Maybe we just hadn't found the right thing to throw. The only one who could be friends with a bear who'd never throw a paving stone at him was sitting right next to me, stroking a cloth picture book that he couldn't read—an angel with no eyes.

"Lunch is ready," Catherine said, calling me to the table. She had prepared beef steaks, chips and a salad of Batavian lettuce. It was like a set meal at a cafe. Catherine placed her chair where she could keep an eye on David in the full-length mirror. We began eating, and I found myself almost inhaling the food ravenously, myself now little more than a dull-witted bear. I hadn't had any meat for two days. I tore the bread—the same kind that Catherine had given us the other day—spreading the mustard that had been served with the beef on it and gobbling it down. I told Catherine that I guess I was starved and that this meal was exactly what I'd really wanted and that it was delicious, all the while shovelling it in. Catherine said with an embarrassed smile that all she'd done was cook some meat and fry some chips from the freezer. She watched, bemused, as I demolished the whole lot in the blink of an eye, then said she'd made a dessert. I said I'd love some, but that she should finish her own meal first. Catherine hadn't eaten half of what was on her plate, so she shrugged, and replied that she probably should. She continued eating, alternating between mouthfuls of meat, chips and vegetables, all the while stealing glances at the mirror.

"I'm taking David for his regular check-up this afternoon. He loves being in the car, and he's always in such a good mood on check-up day. He can feel the wind, hear sounds outside the window, it's like he can 'see'."

Catherine asked me about my job, my family, my life in Tokyo and how I met Yann. She didn't seem to believe that we'd met at a pétanque tournament, instead of at university, or on a company training course, or as friends of friends, or by some other more usual means. I guess that was to be expected. Even I think that it's strange. It was a late autumn Sunday, over a decade ago, in a park on the outskirts of Paris. Playing against local retired people, Yann proved himself to be a good thrower. I can still hear the clank of the ball that won the match. It was a tough throw, the jack surrounded by his opponent's balls. Yann's ball came down from a high angle, almost perpendicular, straight on top of his opponent's, knocking it out of the way and taking its place in exactly the same location. Yann was the youngest player at the tournament, and I spoke to him at lunch, trying to compliment him, but struggling with my French. That was how we met, how our friendship started. I wondered why there weren't any photos of pétanque in his collection. Maybe he just liked playing pétanque, and wasn't interested enough in it to take photos of it. Catherine's questions, I realized, were taking me—ever the idle daydreamer—to all sorts of interesting places.

At a break in the conversation, Catherine stood, went into the kitchen and brought out desert, the surface glowing a rich amber. "Homemade tarte Tatin!" she announced.

She then brought out espresso—the perfect accompaniment for apple tart.

I was full of anticipation, practically salivating, but the instant I bit into a piece, I felt a pain so sharp it was as if my jaw were falling off. I scrunched up my face in agony, and in that instant I was taken back to the suburbs of Paris on a warm spring afternoon, in Yann's studio after a game of pétanque. I'd let slip that I was feeling a bit peckish, so Yann was poking around in the fridge.

"It'll take a while, but I could bake a cake. Fancy it?"

"You'll be the one baking, right?"

"Of course."

"Then I'll try it."

He placed a bunch of carrots to the table, along with a cutting board, a peeler and a knife.

"Chop these up, nice and fine," he said.

"You're not doing it yourself?"

"Come on, you can help."

I peeled the carrots, sliced them, then chopped them into small pieces. In the meantime, Yann had covered about half the table in a mountain of white flour. At the top of the mountain, he dug a little pond into which he cracked some eggs and added butter that had been cut into small cubes. He kneaded the mixture before dumping in about eighty per cent of the carrots I'd chopped. He added in some sugar, dropping it all in one go, as though he were sweetening a cup of North African mint tea. I was worried he'd put too much in. He kneaded the mixture lightly, and skilfully spread it out, creating a fairly thick dough, then put the mixture into a tin with a removable base. He sprinkled the rest of the carrots and more sugar on to the top, then slipped it into the preheated oven. I was very impressed, and I told him so.

"My grandmother taught me how to do it. She used to run a pâtisserie," he replied.

The kitchen was on the mezzanine level, and from the window I could see an old Peugeot in the automotive repair shop across the street, raised above the garage floor. I watched as the bearded mechanic worked under the car, wrench in hand. He lowered the car, and I could hear him revving up the engine. There was no way I could smell the exhaust that was coming out, but after twenty minutes I was sure I could detect a whiff of it in the air, mingling with something sweet and pleasant. It was an uneasy mix of smells.

"It's done," Yann said, carrying over the freshly baked cake, "but we have to let it cool a little first." Yann started to make a pot of tea, but I couldn't wait. Behind his back I cut a small slice and sneaked a few crumbs, and it was exactly as I nibbled on them that it happened. The hot sweetness of the cake penetrated deep into the nerve of my bad molar, and I felt a spasm of pain that ran all the way down my spine. I had to press both hands against my jaw, burying my cheeks in my palms. I crouched down in my chair, in fear.

"Are you all right? What's wrong?" I could hear Yann asking.

"It's my tooth... my tooth," I moaned, barely managing to get the words out.

Yann kept asking me if I was OK, but how could I say I was OK. The pain was intense. My mouth throbbed. It felt like a wire had been yanked through my tooth. My eyes were burning. Tears were rolling down my cheeks.

That was when Yann spotted the crumbs on the table.

"Aha! Serves you right for sneaking a bite," he said, laughing.

"What happened? Are you all right?" It was Catherine's voice. I didn't have any strength in me to reply. Time had flowed backwards, from my pained lower jaw towards the invisible centre of the nervous system, where everything comes together.

THE SANDMAN
IS COMING

SHE WAS WEARING A STRAW HAT with a wide brim, her thin arms at her sides. The little girl, who was holding her hand, was wearing beach sandals decorated with a large bright-pink sponge flower that concealed the strap. She walked a bit unsteadily. She didn't look up at her mother or at the sea, but down at the sand, as though she were scrutinizing it. Something caught her attention, and she stopped in her tracks and crouched down, still holding on to her mother's hand. Her mother had to quickly thrust her right foot forward to keep from being yanked backwards. This brought a shadow over her face.

There were clouds passing overhead, so the sun was not as hot as it could have been. I was sweating anyway. In the distance, where the milky sky seemed to melt into the white sand, the halo of sun made my sleep-deprived eyes tingle. It was a weekday afternoon, and there was almost no one around. Apart from the three of us, there was only an older man walking his dog along the shore. It was a puppy, maybe a Shiba, with a black crease between its eyes, and it looked so friendly and playful that the lead was probably unnecessary. I drew the girl's attention to the dog. She watched as it played in the water, leaping back on to the beach every time a wave approached, then she turned her eyes upwards to me.

"Drink water?" she asked.

"Who?"

"Doggy. Doggy drink water?"

"Hmm. I'm not sure about that. Do you know what seawater tastes like?"

"Tastes salty. Miss Yoko says so."

Miss Yoko was probably a teacher at the nursery she'd started attending that spring. All our conversations proceeded under the assumption that I knew everyone she knew.

"Right. Well, I don't think he'd really gulp it down or anything. He's just getting his nose wet."

"If doggy drink seawater, then doggy get thirsty."

Her mother, who had been listening to our conversation, managed a smile that seemed like a smile. In a voice that was quite like her daughter's, despite being an octave lower, she said that when she was a little girl, she always thought it strange that fish didn't get thirsty. Then she turned to me and said, wasn't it odd she'd forgotten about that? She wanted me to say something back, but

I refrained from the platitude of how it must have been the fresh sea air that had just caused her to remember. If she'd been someone else, the breezes and smell of the sea might have had the effect of letting her relax. But I knew better—I knew she hated the sea and stayed away.

I wasn't being considerate. Filling the gap between emotion and action with "consideration" or "thoughtfulness" was the attitude of someone who tried to be all things to all people, someone whose actions were part of a pattern. My actions were thoughtless, and if praise came my way for that, I'd be grateful and encouraged. On the other hand, if someone were to respond to such praise by saying, "Oh, it's nothing", I'd want to walk the other way. The idea of doing for others what you want done for yourself is, when I think about it, moral and gracious, and I may be well-disposed to it, but it's also a self-pleasuring act. Not doing to others what you don't want done to yourself is no different perhaps, but in this case, given what I knew, I thought it best to keep my mouth shut.

She was the much younger sister of a close friend of mine, and I'd met her the summer after my first year in university. From the first day when she wrapped her sticky hand around my little finger and let me lead her along the beach near her parents' house in Boso, we almost always hung out together, with or without her brother. I wouldn't go as far as to say she felt like a sister, but she definitely felt like a niece. I was twenty and she was six, and that was eighteen years ago. She was just a couple of years older than the little girl staring at the sand in front of me now. Of course, there is a world of difference between a four-year-old and a six-year-old, and back then the six-year-old talked to me all day long, her mouth and hands constantly moving as she played on the beach, building sandcastles that were taller than she was. To keep them from getting washed away by the tide, she'd build further up on the beach, where the sand was hard and she needed a metal spade to dig it out. She'd be completely engrossed in building a castle and the entire town that surrounded it. My friend was still healthy then, and he and I would help by digging the moats. She'd get quite dirty from the wet sand, but she didn't care at all—she just played and played till the sun went down.

Every summer holiday after that, even after she'd become old enough for cleavage to start showing, she would slip into the navy blue swimsuit she wore in the school pool and come with us to the beach. She'd talk passionately about that first sandcastle we built, and as though it were a ritual—or an obligation—we'd build another one. She once overheard me telling her brother that I thought it was funny for a girl to be so interested in such a thing, instead of, say, swimming or tossing a beach ball—or flirting with boys. She responded by saying that there had to be a sand festival somewhere, like the snow festival in Sapporo, and that there had to be a sandcastle world championship, which she definitely wanted to enter. She spoke softly, which led me to question how serious she was, but there was strength and determination in her eyes. I've never forgotten the expression

THE SANDMAN IS COMING

on her face. For several summers after that, she would invite her brother and me to the beach to help her build sandcastles—although it was also to give her brother, who had been spending more and more time in the hospital, a rare day out and the chance to breathe some sea air. She'd make photocopies of European castles, and would even draw rough designs in a sketchbook. Her favourites were the old *châteaux* of France, and she would study the castles of the Loire valley in travel guides, using them as a model for her own turreted replicas. Once I suggested that if we were going to build a castle, we should build a model out of cardboard—it was a waste to build a castle from sand and have it crumble before the night was through. She resisted this suggestion stubbornly. She said that watching as something you'd worked so hard to build came crashing down at high tide was one of the things she enjoyed the most.

EVERY NOW AND AGAIN, I could hear the sound of tyres on the rough asphalt of the highway, which ran along the breakwater. On afternoons when there was not much traffic, the sound of the tyres carried further than the sound of the car engines. This drone was overlaid with the sound of waves, and it reached my ears as a low harmony. I called out the little girl's name—it incorporated one character from her mother's name—as though I was her father. She turned to me, removed her hand from her mother's and grabbed mine. It was small and round like a juggler's beanbag. Her other hand was covered in sand. We walked along this way, her mother now in front of us. In places where there was nothing that looked interesting enough to pick up, she'd dig her sandals into the sand and drag them along, tracing our route with two clumsy lines. Every now and then she'd turn around and look at what she'd created, and sometimes the wind would blow and sand would get in her eyes. When this happened, she'd lift my right hand as it held hers, and use the back of it to rub her eyes and face. Maybe she did this because her free hand was dirty—or maybe it was easier than letting go and using her own hand. It made me think I had to have done the same thing myself—walking along with my parents and using one of their hands to scratch my face. The little girl repeated the action a few times, then, possibly because it wasn't effective, let go and scratched her cheek with her own hand. She ran ahead of both her mother and me, and walked in front of us. The beach was probably new and unusual for her. It was totally different from the pristine sandpit at her nursery—there wasn't even any dog or cat mess to worry about there.

The little girl then walked on the gravelly sand near the shoreline, the water coming up to her ankles. Her mother told her to be careful, not to squat, the tide was coming in, but enticed by the prospect of a seashell, she promptly forgot and squatted and soaked the white underpants that were poking out from under her flower-patterned yellow dress.

"Don't worry," her mother said. "I've brought a change of clothes. But don't grab those seashells. You'll cut yourself."

Pieces of glass that had washed up on to the beach had been worn round and smooth by the sand and the sea, so they weren't a concern, but some seashells were broken in ways that left them with sharp, serrated edges that could really hurt a little girl's soft fingers.

"I should never have given her that *sakura-gai* seashell I found at my parents' house," the girl's mother said. "As soon as I gave it to her, she asked me where I'd got it from. You know, it looked so fragile, I thought it would crumble if I held it too tightly. Remember when I was a girl? There were *sakura-gai* everywhere, you didn't have to look very hard to find them."

When she was a girl... When was that? How many years ago? How old would she have been? I remembered that she'd collected seashells in a wooden box that was for keeping insects. The thin, translucent fragments looked like they'd just fallen off the delicate fingers of a pubescent girl. She'd lined the box with cotton wool and arranged the fingernail-shaped shells as though they were examples of manicure treatments. I found myself glancing at her fingers.

"Anyway, as soon as I told her where the seashell had come from, she insisted on coming here. I was in such a rush when I was packing the bag, I forgot the plasters."

"Telling her to be careful because you forgot the plasters doesn't seem fair..."

"It sure does," she said, and laughed. When she laughed, her lower jaw thrust forward a little, and her protruding lower lip became more noticeable. Her dimples, which were less like hollows and more like little canyons, were as I'd always remembered. Her daughter had inherited her mother's features.

"I think there's a convenience store on the side of the main road. Why don't I go and buy some there, if you're worried about it?"

"There's no need to do that. But thanks."

She said "thanks" in a peculiar way—truncating the word and flinging it at the person who'd done her the kindness. In general, it's difficult to say "thank you" without making it seem like you're hoping for more. Her "thanks" was an exception to this, and I realized that I hadn't heard it for a long time. I'd spent the three years before her brother died living abroad, and we hadn't seen each other during that time. She'd graduated from high school and, after giving up on going to university for financial reasons, had attended a technical school for surveyors while working part-time. When her brother told me that her studies included producing plans and blueprints, the image that came to mind was her favourite Maruman sketchbook, with its orange and green cover, in which she used to draw her sandcastle designs. In fact, according to her brother, she had no interest in real building sites—it seemed she loved her involvement at the abstract stage, but not further. This seemed a pretty self-limiting attitude for a creative person, but there was no doubt that she meant it sincerely.

However, towards the end of her first year at this technical school—a time when I thought she'd be developing her skills—she dropped out and got married. It was a quick decision, and her parents had barely any time to object. Her husband was an architect, who had been an occasional lecturer at the school. He was ten years older than she was, and he'd spent years living on various islands, supervising the construction of seawalls—his speciality was flood control. I don't know how he explained his background to her, but she'd always been a bit of a dreamer and he reeled her in easily enough, persuading her to leave school. They moved to the island of Oshima, but as soon as she got pregnant, he suddenly started taking frequent trips to the head office on the mainland. She began to sense the purpose of these trips, and when she realized that this behaviour would not change after the baby was born, she put an end to their relationship, just as quickly as they'd got married in the first place. I knew about all this because my friend had kept in touch, writing to me from his hospital bed that it seemed his sister was operating on a different wavelength from her husband—she liked sandcastles, he liked reinforced concrete. I didn't know about the divorce until I received the official notice of my friend's death, though. I called her after I returned to Japan, but I never mentioned her ex-husband, and she didn't say a word about him either.

The day before had been a Sunday, and I'd come to this seaside town—the first time in a long time—to mark the second anniversary of my friend's death. I'd spent the night drinking with his parents and his hometown friends, and I'd taken today off work, and so his sister, now a woman, invited me to come for a walk on the beach with her daughter. I was still wearing my mourning suit, everything except the jacket and tie. I remembered how my friend had written that when his sister was pregnant, and for a while after the baby was born, she used to spend all her time by the sea. Since the divorce, however, she stayed away, and she'd even stopped visiting her parents, whose home was on the coast. In fact, she'd made the radical decision to move with her daughter to an inland city. This was the first time they'd been back in months.

The little girl began wandering down the beach, away from the man with his dog. Sometimes she'd stop and squat, entranced by something in the sand and picking it up. I couldn't tell if it was seashells or something else. The petal-like pink *sakura-gai* would be washed clean by the waves, and buried in the gravelly sand.

"I'm going over to her," I said. "I'm a little worried about the waves."

There was a pile of charred wood on the sand, where someone had built a fire. I stood next to it and, keeping my eyes on the little girl, I took off my shoes and socks. I tried to roll up my trousers, but ended up losing my balance. As I stumbled about, suddenly I heard my friend's sister gasp from behind me.

"What's the matter?" I asked, turning around quickly.

"It's my earring. It's gone. I must have dropped it somewhere."

She tucked in her chin and tilted her head like a little bird, and with both hands removed the earring from her other ear, and showed it to me. It was a simple thing, several thin fragments of gemstone layered on top of each other to create a petal effect. They were of such an unobtrusive design I hadn't noticed them earlier.

"Did you have it when we came down on to the beach?"

"I'm not sure. Maybe."

"Well, we can try retracing our steps. It's not going to be easy, though. The colour of the earring is so subtle, it'll blend in with the sand. But let's go back and look."

I ran down to the little girl and explained that Mummy had dropped something and that we needed to help her find it. I took her hand and then the three of began our search effort. As luck would have it, the little girl had been dragging her sandals all the way along and it was easy to see the path we'd taken. The area we had to cover was therefore confined, which meant that we actually had a chance of finding the earring. We were bending over, eyes concentrating, hardly saying a word, as though we were in a competition to see who could find it first. As we got away from the shore, there were fewer shells and more rubbish and dry seaweed. We used sticks to poke around, and to stir through the sand where our three sets of footprints crossed each other. Sometimes our sticks would knock into each other, as though we were in battle, and sometimes this would prove so funny that we'd break out laughing.

"You think this is anything like the treasure hunt on the Magdalen Islands?" my friend's sister asked out of the blue.

"What? Where?"

"You wrote to me about it? In a letter from France?"

"Did I?"

"Well, it was a letter to my brother actually. He let me read it. He thought you might want him to share it with me. Sorry if he shouldn't have..."

"Heh. It's a bit late to apologize now."

"It sure is," she said with a smile. "You wrote something about sandcastles too. Do you remember that?"

I did have some memory of writing to my friend about those islands. I hadn't gone there myself—an acquaintance, who spent every summer in Nantucket, "the whaling capital of the world", had told me stories about his visit. The Magdalen Islands are part of Quebec, and there are two ways to get there: you can either take a boat from Quebec City or Montreal down the Saint Lawrence River out into the Gulf of Saint Lawrence, or you can cross over to Newfoundland from New Brunswick and take a ship that goes via Prince Edward Island—which is where *Anne of Green Gables* is set. The economy of the Islands is mainly centred on fishing and tourism, and each summer they hold a treasure hunt, which is based on local history, as well as a sandcastle competition. My acquaintance had taken part in both. The treasure hunt had a generous prize, but he said the sandcastle contest was much more fun and "just crazy, man". There were these wonderful intricately constructed sandcastles—"they're just huge". They'd been holding the competition for decades, and there were several different categories—for children, adults, families, and according to theme. But unlike the Sapporo snow festival, where you could build anything you liked, everyone had to build a castle.

My acquaintance entered the "hard labour" category where a team of adults had to build a castle that was at least a metre high in the space of a day. Planks and containers could be used, but no adhesives, just water. The teams had practised together just for the competition, so the standard of the constructions was really impressive. My acquaintance showed me photos: a Tower of Babel with five or six vaulted layers supported by columns; a phantasmagorical castle, covered in Gaudi-inspired elements that looked like threadworms; a soaring Machu Picchu citadel. I thought there was no way people could build things like that just by picturing them in their heads, and my acquaintance said that teams were allowed to bring designs with them.

With the exception of the children's categories, the competition started at eight in the morning and continued until four in the afternoon, when the winner of each category was determined by spectators' vote. The entire event took place just a few metres from the shoreline, with consideration given to high tides and low tides. On this one day of the year, people devoted their lives to building sandcastles. They were not professionals in the field, but people with fanciful visions. They built brilliant castles in the sand that were gone the next day. There was something dreamlike about it.

I'd written all this to my friend in the hospital because I wanted him to think about travelling to somewhere like the Magdalen Islands, a whole other world where the air was clean and fresh, and then, say, when the time was right, heading south to Nantucket to watch the whales. I dreamed unrealistically, that he could recuperate this way. Anyway, a couple of years later now, thinking about that letter, it stood to reason that he'd let his sister read it—the three of us had built sandcastles together, after all.

"I remember thinking how I really wanted to go there someday."

"We could take your daughter when she's a bit older."

"Just the three of us?"

"Is there anyone else?"

She was silent.

"Let's forget the sandcastles for now. We've got a treasure hunt going on," I said.

We'd walked all the way back to the concrete stairs that led up to the road, and we still hadn't found the lost earring, just a whole load of different seashells. We were tired, so we decided to lay out a plastic sheet and take a break. The little girl couldn't sit still and went to play in the sand behind us. It wasn't long before I heard her distinctive squeal.

"Have you found it?"

"Drinked it!"

"You drank something? What was it? Did you swallow it?"

"The doggy drinked the sea! Drinked the sea and made a funny face!"

The older man with the dog, seeing that we had headed away from the shore, had let it off its lead, letting it run free. Not that the dog was interested in running anywhere. Instead of jumping in and out of the water, it barely strayed more than a few feet from its owner, and seemed content to thrust its snout into the damp sand. Had the little girl seen it lapping up some water? I thought she'd been down on her hands and knees in the sand, but who knows where children are looking. I asked her what kind of funny face the dog had made.

"Doggy sticked face in the sea, then squished up its nose!"

"Its face got all wrinkly, did it?"

"Face said it was salty!"

"I bet it did."

The dog had been thirsty so now the little girl was too. Her mother pulled a bottle of mineral water out of her rucksack and handed it to her.

We sat there, my senses picking up the feel and smell of the sea breeze. My ears were filled with the sound of the waves.

"It's a shame we don't have any beer. Here, you can have some of this, if you like," the little girl's mother said, handing me a plastic bottle of oolong tea.

I took a sip, then spluttered, "It's salty!" I looked at the little girl as I grimaced. She looked shocked to the core.

"I give you water. Drink this," she said.

I suppose jokes are a kind of language only for people past a certain age. Still, I couldn't tell her I'd been faking, so I poured a tiny amount of the mineral water into the blue plastic cap of the bottle, making as exaggerated a performance of washing the taste away as I could possibly manage.

"Better?"

"All better now. Thank you."

"Should give water to doggy too."

The dog, who'd expressed his displeasure at drinking the salty water by wrinkling his brow, had followed its owner around to the other side of the rocks. They were heading for the next beach along. All I could see was the back of the dog standing still, its tail wagging up in the air, like a brush. This brought to mind another thing about the sandcastle tournament in the Magdalen Islands that my acquaintance had told me. Apart from the competitors in official categories, there were freelancers who built really ingenious stuff like a complete set of household furnishings, or an entire zoo. He had photos of the beach crawling with dogs, crocodiles, hippos, all with such life-like expressions it was hard to believe they were made of sand. There was even a giraffe that supposedly was one-metre tall—not including the neck!

How handy it would be if seashells and earrings could be created on demand, I mused to myself. I lay down on my back, looking up at the sky, my legs extended past the plastic sheet. I didn't care if I got sand on my borrowed mourning clothes. My gaze turned towards the little girl's mother. I could see grains of sand on her slender neck. In the next moment a strong breeze sent a spray of sand towards me, and I squeezed my eyes shut. I started thinking about the comforting expression "The Sandman is coming"—*Le marchand de sable est passé*—and the next thing I knew I was drifting off. I have no idea how long I slept.

As I opened my eyes, the first thing I saw was the soles of two feet, almost in my face. They were quivering slightly. I propped myself up, and the girl's mother turned towards me. She'd taken off her hat and tied up her hair. It seemed she hadn't changed in all the time we'd known each other.

"Good morning," she said to me.

"Good morning," her daughter imitated her.

"Fancy giving us a hand? If you're up to it, that is."

Mother and daughter were building a sandcastle. A small cone had already been formed, encircled by a moat that was about twenty centimetres deep. "We need to hurry—before the tide comes in," she said with a smile. Suddenly she didn't look like a mother. She looked like a woman in her mid-twenties.

"You're not worried about her getting hurt any more? Not having any plasters and all?" I asked, mostly in jest.

She confirmed that everything was fine, then returned to her task. From where I sat, it occurred to me how her figure seemed rather like an ant's, her upper torso wide, her waist very narrow, her hips wider, and time suddenly became warped.

IT'S FINE FOR YOU, YES? To stay here with us a little longer. You're going back to Tokyo tonight, right? So this is the only chance we have."

She was fifteen, and her cleavage was dusted in sand. As usual, she'd cut out a photo of a medieval French castle from a travel magazine and spread it out on the beach, and she was asking her brother and me to help her build it. We gave her our opinion that it would be impossible to build such a castle, but she wouldn't listen. She'd brought a camera to photograph the end product, and she was determined to get it done. In the end we were construction workers creating a replica of Carcassonne, complete with towers positioned equal distances apart and sturdy walls dotted with embrasures. It was noon by the time we started, and the tide was rising. We had to rush, keeping one eye on the sea all the while.

It got to be just like she said. Creating something that we knew would be destroyed was giving us an unexplainable sense of accomplishment that was the opposite of transience, and it was a spur for me as well as for her brother, who must have already been carrying the illness inside him. If we were going to recreate a medieval castle, marking out the plot in the sand and then surrounding it with a moat was the easy part—but if we did that first, we wouldn't be able to get inside of the castle and build all the parts there. Better to build the main part of the castle first, I said, the part that was like the keep of a Japanese castle, then stabilize it before moving on to the walls and then the moat. But we had to do it her way. She created an enclosure that guessed at the size of the finished castle. She tiptoed, bending over like a flamingo in the tight space, scrunching up her body as she formed the towers and walls. Her hips and buttocks, which had not yet found their shape, flashed in front of me, very close. I remember the surprise I felt as though it was yesterday. I might have been digging a bit too enthusiastically and sliced open my middle finger on a broken seashell. I washed the sand away in the seawater, and pressed a tissue hard against the wound until the blood stopped. She then wrapped a plaster that had a cartoon character on it around my finger.

When I stood up, I felt a little faint from lying in the sun. The tide was coming in, the waves beginning to crash against the shore. I walked down to the sea, washed sand off my hands and scooped some water to splash on my face. I looked down, and saw, among the fine black and brown gravel shifting in the waves, a pale shard. I thrust my hands into the gravel, trying to grab hold of it, but the next wave came along suddenly and carried the beautiful pink fingernail of a shell away. A loud sigh escaped me, and as I turned around, I saw a woman who was once again a fifteen-year-old girl. Her lips, dusted with sand, looked like a fingernail. A crescent moon.

IN THE
OLD CASTLE

THE ENVELOPE CONTAINED A LETTER, folded into quarters, and a single black-and-white photograph, which was out of focus. A man was sitting on a chair that had been wedged into a narrow-domed niche in a stone wall. He'd had to hunch his shoulders to fit. His left hand was on his knee, and his right hand, index finger extended, was pointing upwards. The cheap flash had made his stubble-covered face contrast so unnaturally with his surroundings that it seemed to float out of the frame, like the head of a wax doll. His eyes were wide open, staring straight into the camera lens, no sign of averting his gaze. There was no mistaking who this man was. The half-smile on the right side of the mouth could only have belonged to me, and though it was rare that I took off my glasses off in public, my face was unmistakable. I was much thinner than I am now, with sallow, sickly looking cheeks. I stared at the photo for a while, as though it was a picture of a complete stranger. Then I started reading the letter, which had been written with a blue pen.

"I bet this photo will come as a surprise, after all this time," the sender had written. "Do you remember when you came to visit us at our house? It was a long time ago. We spent the day drinking cider, and then you had a little nap. In the evening you and I went for a walk into the hills, up to the old castle..."

I'd met my friend, who was a little older than me, through my work as a translator. One day—it must have been ten years ago—he invited me to come and visit him at his home in Normandy. I took him up on his offer, and we agreed on which train I'd take. That seemed to be all the preparation that was required. My plan had been to get cash from the ATM in the station, but when I got there, I realized that I'd completely forgotten about my weekly limit, and I couldn't withdraw enough to cover my ticket. I also couldn't use my credit card unless the purchase was over a hundred francs, and my cheque account had insufficient funds. I was effectively almost penniless. Fortunately, I had just enough cash on me for a one-way journey, but it was an inauspicious start that left me feeling a bit despondent. Still, everything went fine at first. As soon as the platform of my train was displayed, I walked through the ticket gate and boarded. I found a seat on the right side of the carriage, then remembered how, the previous night, my friend had gone on at length, saying I should sit on the left. I was about to get up and change my seat when I heard some excited voices, and before I knew it there were German pensioners everywhere—and not only in my compartment. It seemed they'd taken over the whole carriage. So I stayed put. Beer and snacks were now being passed back and forth, and as the train pulled away from the station, guttural sounds filled my ears. I had the unworthy thought that I needed only some sauerkraut and sausages to open a German pub.

An older woman, who'd sat down next to me, opened up a tourist brochure—apparently the group were going to visit the home of a famous Impressionist painter, which included a museum and his famous gardens. It was clear from the way she chatted with her friends that everyone was quite excited about the excursion.

Surrounded by large Germans, which made me feel squeezed into my seat, I tried my best to ignore the barrage of consonants. At some point I fell asleep, dozing until some commotion woke me up. We'd arrived at the station where the Germans were to get off, but the compartment door wouldn't open and the travellers were trapped inside. A red-faced older man was pushing down on the door handle, banging on the glass and shouting for someone to let them out. It was the franticness in his voice that snapped me awake. Since I'd been on a French train before, I knew to tell the man that he needed to pull the handle up, instead of pushing it down. My intervention didn't go very well, however, and in the end the conductor had to come around to resolve the problem. I had been no help whatsoever, and the entire group rushed past me without a word of thanks. I didn't feel especially worthy of gratitude, but there was a part of me that felt that I should have got something for my trouble. Nevertheless, my attention soon shifted to the question of whether my friend, who was useless at keeping promises, would actually be waiting to meet me at the station. And also whether his girlfriend had been able to take the day off work to be there too. He'd finally met "the one", he said, and he was eager to introduce me to her.

It turned out I needn't have been concerned. At my stop, only a handful of people got on or off the train, and I saw my friend right away, with his unshaven cheeks and his year-round uniform of jeans and cotton shirt, standing next to a woman who was about a head taller than him. She was clearly over forty, and was wearing no make-up. Her clothes were so shabby that I almost felt sorry for her—a stained STOP AIDS T-shirt, light brown trousers clinging tightly to bulging buttocks, with back pockets turned inside out, looking like rabbit ears. My friend introduced us, we kissed each other on both cheeks, and the three of us were soon talking like we were old friends. I felt content to be in the company of a cheerful woman. It felt like it had been a while.

The route from the station to where they lived took us along many roads, including one elegantly lined with trees. We passed farms where cows stood in clusters of two or three—a picture of pastoral bliss. As we got closer to the city, such scenes were replaced by supermarkets with giant car parks and traditional stone houses interspersed with modern residential developments. It was an uneven townscape that made me feel quite uncomfortable.

Their house was new, on the outskirts of town, and had been built according to a model that allowed for a minimum of comfort. The kitchen, with fitted sink, was immediately on the left as soon as you walked through the front door, washing machine and refrigerator slotted in next to each other, uniform in height. There was a toilet and bath in a room spacious enough to be mistaken for storage. There was also a bedroom, lined with wardrobes fitted with enormous mirrored doors and a bed so big there was barely floor space. The main room of the house was about twenty-five square metres and had no built-ins. Instead, the walls were lined with home-made shelves.

We went out into the garden and sat at the table there, gulping down large glasses of strong-smelling cider from a local farm. The neighbour's cat crawled under the hedge to join us. We talked about anything and everything. They told me how they'd got together. At some point, I crashed on the sofa, and my friend and his girlfriend went out to buy food for dinner. By the time they came back, it was already past five.

"I'm going to make a tart for dessert. Which would you like—rhubarb or raspberries?" the girlfriend asked me.

"Rhubarb," I answered without hesitation. It was the right answer—she apparently loved cooking the stuff, and loved the taste too. While she prepared our meal, my friend suggested we go for a walk to the old castle that was being restored in the hills behind their house. As he explained, the pile of rubble that everyone had ignored for years had recently been identified as the residence of an eminent archbishop. This discovery had caused something of an uproar, and the place was suddenly enjoying a great deal of attention.

After passing through the winding streets of the old town, we stopped to buy cigarettes at the only cafe that was open, then turned down a narrow path between two houses. Eventually we reached the wood, where the soil was mouldy, rather like compost. The distinctively fine rain of this region mingled with the soil to create an aroma that you could almost taste—sweet, tangy. The path seemed well trodden, and was snugly enveloped in a tunnel of brush. A fragment of a rainbow was visible through the early summer leaves. We aimed for the top of the hill, frantically driving our creaky knees ever onwards, occasionally taking a break to sit on a fallen tree and talking in short bursts.

My friend had always had trouble finding a girlfriend, and it was an unexpected series of events that got him to be in this position—cohabiting with someone who was not only ten years older, but who also had, in her own words, "already done the marriage thing". The reason they'd decided to live in a place so inconvenient was because she worked in a bookshop in a nearby city. Living here also meant that he could spend time with his seven-year-old niece.

My friend had doted on his niece ever since she was a toddler. One of the tales he liked to tell involved the first time she'd been taken to church to attend a wedding, when she'd broken the joyful yet solemn silence to ask her mother if the priest believed in God. My friend was living with his sister's family back then, and his niece had almost motherly concern about her uncle. "Everyone else is in a couple. Why are you all alone?" she'd ask, whenever they saw each other. When he finally met his girlfriend and introduced his niece to her, his niece's response was not what he had expected: "Her belly sticks out a bit, but you're making progress!" This unaffected declaration caused my friend's slightly plump girlfriend to freeze for a moment, but she burst out laughing after the child had been scolded. The following morning the little girl had been given permission to go and wake the couple, who were sharing a room. She must have got shy, however, because she couldn't bring herself to knock on the door. Instead she fidgeted, unsure of herself. My friend's girlfriend could hear the niece walking back and forth, and without doing anything to her hair or putting on any make-up, opened the door to wish the little girl good morning.

A few days later, the niece was at school, learning how to use the word "surprising". In her composition she wrote: "When my uncle's girlfriend came out of their room in the morning and her hair was really messy, it was surprising." Her parents were summoned to an official meeting with the teacher.

"What's surprising is that she could compose such an eloquent sentence," I said, unable to stop myself.

"You're taking her side?" my friend said, amused. "Now *that* is surprising..."

Still it was clear from that he adored his niece. She also shared the cheerful, open nature of his girlfriend. After all, this woman in her stained T-shirt had put up on their bathroom wall a Benetton poster featuring rows of men's genitals, and would study them from all angles, telling me with a laugh that every day she tried to decide which genitals were her boyfriend's. There was something heroic about her. From my point of view, girlfriend and niece were equally surprising.

We left the clearing from where we could look out over the town, and I followed my friend as he strode through a tunnel of greenery that he'd nicknamed the "royal road". We emerged at the back of the castle grounds. Nightfall was beginning, but I could see that about half of the castle remained untouched by the restoration.

The ground around the castle was wet from the fine rain that had been falling. One side of the tower was missing, and its roof had worn smooth over the centuries. Reconstruction of the south-facing facade was almost complete, but everything else still looked like a building site. Work had apparently been delayed not only because of the sheer scale of the castle and the inevitable financial difficulties, but also because of differing views regarding what shape the final reconstruction should take. According to my friend, it was decided, following a consultation with the public, that the restored castle should recreate the original building as faithfully as possible.

The castle was overseen by a groundskeeper, who lived in a bungalow on the edge of the wood.

"He's a tall guy, thin, with a sharp look in his eyes. In his late fifties, probably. He's got a Doberman, which looks miserable," my friend said with a grimace. "Of course, it'd be a different story if the owner treated it properly. They're really intelligent dogs, but the groundskeeper treats it like a mutt. He keeps it in this kennel next to the bungalow, and never takes it for walks or anything. He used to let it loose on the grounds after all the visitors left, but he can't do that any more."

"Did the dog ever go after anyone? I mean, considering that he'd been cooped up all day."

"Strangely enough, that never happened. He did chase me once, though. Stubborn old coot, he didn't give up easily. Kept cursing at me..."

"The Doberman did?"

"Don't be ridiculous. The groundskeeper, obviously. He had the dog with him. You should have seen the look on his face, it was like he owned this place. Like he had a divine right to be here or something. I mean, he really does sort of think that. They say he turned the president away once."

The story my friend told went like this: Back when the reconstruction work was less than half finished, an older gentleman brought a group of people to the castle, and told the groundskeeper that he wanted to show them this wonderful cultural relic. The groundskeeper, failing to recognize this gentleman as the president, told him that the castle was off-limits, and that it couldn't be visited without permission from the Town Hall. When someone in the entourage explained that the groundskeeper was speaking to the President of the French Republic, the groundskeeper stood firm. "Presidents, of all people, should set an example by getting the proper permission from the Town Hall," he said, puffing out his chest. No one knew why he wasn't sacked for this, though it has to be said that his reasoning was faultless.

The still-under-reconstruction castle—a place so hallowed, even the president had not been allowed to visit—was now sinking slowly into the setting sun. The trees that surrounded the castle stirred in the gentle wind, their branches disappearing into a hole in a ruined gable, their hues merging with the those of the interior of the building. Pools of colour were forming a scene that would not have looked out of place among the water lilies of that painter who'd lived in this area. The paving stones were damp, and there were the sounds of a stream. A cool breeze caressed my body, which was now free of the effects of the alcohol I'd drunk earlier.

Entirely predictably, gazing at the scene before me, I got the near-desperate urge to see inside the castle itself. If I missed this chance, I'd probably never be able to do it all again—to be in a town like this, in a landscape like this. I surveyed the wall, and it did not seem insurmountable. And I thought, further, that if the castle was under reconstruction, breaking in wouldn't be difficult. When I revealed this idea to my friend, he lifted his hands with his palms open and, in a childlike voice, said "My uncle's Japanese friend begged him to break into an old castle. It was surprising." My friend smiled, then added, "Actually, I was expecting this to happen."

Clambering over the stone wall was surprisingly easy. I quickly dropped down on the other side and, being careful to step lightly, made my way along the front of the castle to the area where the building materials were stored. I found a window that had been boarded up with a sheet of plywood. From a crack on the side of the window space, I could see a large, high-ceilinged hall that looked like the inner sanctum of a church. Light was leaking in from crevices here and there, so the space was not haunted-house-dark, but something about the crumbling walls made it very foreboding. I was waiting for my friend, my partner in crime, before taking the next step. Where was he?

He was struggling to scale the wall. It seemed I'd neglected to take one thing into account: my friend and I were about the same height, but he weighed one-and-a-half times as much, and the extra kilos were holding him back. Eventually, however, he managed to get some purchase, and dragged himself up. When he did get one leg over to straddle the wall, he broke out into a smile.

He dropped down with a thud to where I was standing. I was worried that someone could have heard that, but he doubted it, full of confidence again. Relieved, I prised open a door that was hanging loose on its hinges, and we slowly proceeded down a corridor towards the tower. It was dusty, but there was no mouldy smell—probably because air was blowing through. We thought there might be a model of the castle in a glass case, or a portrait of the archbishop, or something, but there was nothing worth spending time on. Eventually, we found the stairs to the tower and started to climb. About halfway up, a landing led to a small room, which we stepped into. In the far wall there was a niche and in it was a stool, similar to those used by staff at art galleries. My friend, his mischievous nature roused, attempted to get in and sit on it, only to find the niche too narrow. I gave it a try, and just about managed it by hunching down. Having achieved that much, I decided to go the whole hog, removing my glasses and posing like a saint for my friend's amusement. Pulling a camera out of his rucksack, he stepped backwards in order to frame this icon, then clicked the shutter which fired off the flash. Blue-white light filled the room, and in the next instant we heard a man's booming voice, so loud it seemed to cause the entire castle to shake. I found myself shrivelling up in the niche.

"What the hell are you doing!?" barked the grounds-keeper. The flash must have lit up the stairwell too.

My friend was caught where he stood, camera in hand, totally surprised, frozen to the spot. But because I was wedged into the niche, I could not see the groundskeeper, nor could he see me.

"I saw you! I saw you climbing over the wall!" the groundskeeper said, his voice full of menace.

"I'm really very sorry," my friend responded earnestly. "I just thought the town would look really beautiful from up here in the evening light."

I didn't know how he'd learned to be such a smooth talker. He gave nothing away, and acted as if he was alone as he walked up to the groundskeeper and made his way towards the exit. I decided to stay put for a bit, but fear of the Doberman seized me and I started trembling. Then I worried that if I managed to escape from the castle, I'd never be able to find my way home. I thought of the rhubarb tart that would go uneaten. I worried I'd die alone in the darkness. I cursed my luck at being unable to withdraw any cash in the morning—I could have bribed the groundskeeper. I strained to hear footsteps. Should I just go and turn myself in? Would the groundskeeper let my friend go? This was a man who'd faced down the President of France. Would he turn my friend over to the police?

I could hear traces of conversation between my friend and the groundskeeper and convinced myself that they were on the other side of the outer wall. Somehow that was reassuring, so despite its being probably more risky than taking a picture with a flash, I lit a cigarette. I decided to wait in the tower for a while. Twenty, thirty minutes passed, and my friend still had not come to get me. It was getting darker and darker, and with no sign of life in the early summer countryside. I thought of those old Germans with their crunching consonants, and wondered if they got to see the blues and greens and purples of the branches that drooped on to the serene surface of the pond. No matter how familiar it was, the paintings of those water lilies contained the purest, most tranquil light ever created by a human being. If only I'd gone with the Germans, I'd be immersed in dazzling colours, instead of being stuck in some dusty, dark crevice. I needed to get out of the castle quickly.

I tiptoed along the corridor, feeling my way against the wall. Once outside, I avoided the gravel, following a path that had some grass on it. I found the spot where we'd climbed over the wall. I stopped, listening hard for anything, anyone. There was only quiet, so I climbed the wall and as soon as I landed on the other side, I started running at full speed down through the tunnel of greenery back the way we'd come. The incline of the slope caused my knees to wobble, and I worried about the dangers of running in the darkness. Then suddenly I saw a faint halo of orange light ahead of me. I slowed down, relieved, and walked towards it, discovering that it was a street light illuminating concrete steps with a handrail. I started to run down the steps, sensing freedom at last, but what was waiting for me at the bottom was an iron gate, a kind of portcullis.

The game was up. I was trapped. I looked up into the pitch-black sky, in despair. Then out of the darkness, I could hear something. A quiet voice. And then a faint light. Dimly I made out my friend carrying a torch. His girlfriend was with him. Half-weeping, I called out his name, and grabbed on to the iron bars, shaking them, like a prisoner imploring a jailer he cannot see. "Open it," I cried, just like the Germans who had been trapped in the train compartment. "Please, open it." It was as though I was trying to escape from every single unpleasant memory that humanity had ever experienced.